flat-line statch...

He stopped less than an arm's length away, and instantly the space between them crackled with heat. The grooves in his mind slotted back into blistering memories of last night and the undeniable force that clawed at him whenever she was near.

He set his jaw. Got a grip. Slapped that mental wall back up.

'Nina, you can't continue to work here.'

Her slim nostrils flared before she slowly nodded. 'I understand. I do.' She glanced over their cold meals. 'If it's all the same with you, I won't stay for dinner.'

She turned and, as his throat and chest burned, walked through into the main room.

Cursing under his breath, he strode off to catch up. This woman would drive him *nuts*.

The pull—this fierce physical attraction—was too strong to ignore. No matter how many times she walked away he would have to bring her back. Because what he'd tried to block from his mind all the long day *would* happen. He knew it as

The ... e'd
bett

Dear Reader

Remember the movie *Sliding Doors*? Sometimes a closing door can be a blessing in disguise!

My heroine in FIRED WAITRESS, HIRED MISTRESS harks from a prestigious background. From a young age Nina Petrelle has expected, and received, the best of everything. Gabe Steele, on the other hand, comes from humble stock. Despite the difference in family bank balances, Gabe was Nina's brother's best mate. Fourteen-year-old Nina couldn't pinpoint why Gabe's dismissive behaviour towards her should rankle so much, but she evened the score by jibing Gabe about his station in life every chance she got.

Then those doors slapped shut.

When Nina's father died, ultimately so did the Petrelle fortune. Nina, who would have continued along her privileged path, now struggles to meet bills. Conversely, the tragedy that struck Gabe's world set a fire beneath his determination to succeed. It is as a cool, wealthy playboy that he meets Nina again.

A more mature and modest Nina scorns the hedonistic world in which Gabe now reigns supreme. Gabe, however, knows Nina is simply cut over their changed circumstances: beneath her waitress garb she's still that spoilt brat. As mismatched as they were in the past, they are doubly so now. Yet neither can deny the explosive magnetism which, time and again, draws them together and fights to keep them close.

Life is a series of twists and turns. When one door shuts, another will surely open. But travelling a new road isn't always easy—particularly where pride and love are concerned.

Hope you enjoy FIRED WAITRESS, HIRED MISTRESS!

Warmest wishes

Robyn

FIRED WAITRESS, HIRED MISTRESS

BY
ROBYN GRADY

MILLS & BOON®
MODERN
Heat™

All the characters in this book have no existence outside the imagination of the author, and have no relation whatsoever to anyone bearing the same name or names. They are not even distantly inspired by any individual known or unknown to the author, and all the incidents are pure invention.

First published in Great Britain 2010
Harlequin Mills & Boon Limited,
Eton House, 18-24 Paradise Road, Richmond, Surrey TW9 1SR

© Robyn Grady 2010

ISBN: 978 0 263 87734 2

Harlequin Mills & Boon policy is to use papers that are natural, renewable and recyclable products and made from wood grown in sustainable forests. The logging and manufacturing process conform to the legal environmental regulations of the country of origin.

Printed and bound in Spain
by Litografia Rosés, S.A., Barcelona

One Christmas long ago, **Robyn Grady** received a book from her big sister and immediately fell in love with Cinderella. Sprinklings of magic, deepest wishes come true—she was hooked! Picture books with glass slippers later gave way to romance novels and, more recently, the real-life dream of writing for Mills & Boon.

After a fifteen-year career in television, Robyn met her own modern-day hero. They live on Australia's Sunshine Coast with their three little princesses, two poodles, and a cat called Tinkie. Robyn loves new shoes, worn jeans, lunches at Moffat Beach and hanging out with her friends on eHarlequin. Learn about her latest releases at www.robyngrady.com, and don't forget to say hi. She'd love to hear from you!

Recent titles by the same author:

Modern Heat™

CONFESSIONS OF A MILLIONAIRE'S MISTRESS
NAUGHTY NIGHTS IN THE MILLIONAIRE'S MANSION
DEVIL IN A DARK BLUE SUIT

Desire™

FOR BLACKMAIL...OR PLEASURE?
BEDDED BY BLACKMAIL

This one's for the mega talented
'209ers RWA Bootcamp' gals! Thanks Rachel, Alison
and Nikki, for organising a great couple of days.
Onward and upward, ladies!

With thanks, as always,
to my fab editor Kimberley Young
for helping to bring out the best in my work.

CHAPTER ONE

FROM the moment Nina Petrelle opened her eyes, she was painfully aware of three things.

One: she had a pounding great bump on the back of her head. Two: her ankle was stuck in what felt like a soggy, splintered vice. Three: cool, salty water was lapping the length of her prostrate body…was filling her mouth *and* her lungs.

Choking on seawater, Nina came fully to. She sat bolt upright and, an instant later, yelped in hair-raising agony. Gritting her teeth, she clutched at her thigh. When the red-tipped arrows firing up her shin gradually eased, Nina withered back down.

But she wouldn't give in to the tears. *Damned* if she would. Instead Nina thumped both fists hard against the sand.

Little by little over the last two months she'd felt tiny pieces of herself falling away. The sense that she was losing the battle kept rubbing and chipping at her strength until this afternoon, after a gruelling shift, she'd fixed her heart upon escape. But what she'd truly wanted to leave behind—the question she didn't want to face—had followed her.

Lately it had haunted her.

Who am I?

She didn't know any more.

Once life had shone out before her like a glittering golden path. Her father had owned a highly successful engineering firm and, growing up, she'd thought nothing of her family's numerous house staff, nor her expectations of having the best clothes, the best food—the best of *everything*. Of course that had been before her father had died, her manic mother had stripped the family coffers clean and her usually responsible kid sister had got pregnant by a deadbeat who hadn't hung around.

While her mother had gone into a tailspin, Nina had pulled up her sleeves. After completing her university degree, she'd landed a job in publishing—a fast-paced, intense world she adored. Until recently she'd worked as the features editor for an acclaimed teen magazine, *Shimmer*.

Then the blunt axe had fallen.

Along with a number of other staff she'd been retrenched. With a sizeable mortgage, and other commitments, she'd needed a job, but well-paid positions weren't so easy to come by, particularly in her field. With everyone tightening their belts, the shrivelled industry grapevine was as quiet as a church.

One morning, while prioritising her mounting bills, a long-time friend had called. Alice Sully's family owned a travel agency and, if Nina was desperate, her dad could wangle her a stint working on an exclusive holiday retreat; he knew the owner. Waitressing hours there would be long, Alice had warned her, but the money was great.

Slumping with relief, Nina had accepted, and these past six weeks she'd worked her butt off at Diamond Shores, Australia's premier Great Barrier Reef resort.

And not one moment went by when she didn't wish herself back home.

Most of the other staff had let her know they weren't happy that she'd swung a ticket here via the back door. A job at what many considered Australia's holiday Mecca was supposed to be hard-won, and two years helping part-time at the uni cafeteria didn't make muster.

But, needing the work, she'd been determined to do her best. So she held her head high, when most of the time she felt like a big fat pretender. She smiled till her face ached. Even when pampered patrons accused her of getting their orders wrong. Or commanded her to do silly things, like massage their temples for ridiculous amounts of time if they felt a headache coming on. And that was only the beginning. When she crashed, late at night, her dreams were a jumble of spilled cocktails, tumbling plates and an endless parade of growling, super-rich guests.

That was the hardest.

Once *Nina Petrelle* had lounged on the A list. *She'd* sipped chilled Cristal cocktails and worried about little other than her designer tan, acrylic tips, or the lack of room to accommodate her ever-expanding wardrobe. Now, existing on the other side of the glass wall, that kind of over-indulgence near sickened her. She wanted to shake these out-of-touch squillionaires and let them know there were real people out there and they were doing it tough.

But alongside her indignation lived another emotion. A desire that, in the still dead of night, made Nina's cheeks burn with shame.

Envy.

Secretly she craved to cast off her uniform and rest her weary limbs. She wanted to sprawl out on one of those sunwashed deckchairs and beg, borrow or steal the chance to return to the decadence of her previously worry-free life—if just for a day or two.

She hadn't thought she'd miss extravagance. Had never imagined ever wanting to be a society princess again. She had a *new* life, and obscene luxury simply wasn't her any more.

Yet here she was—torn between opposing self-indulgence and desperately wanting it back.

A monster of a wave crashed on the shore and Nina was brought back to the harrowing present. As the sea rushed in, a cry slipped from her throat, but, with water flooding her windpipe, her "Help!" came out a spluttering cough.

Who would hear anyway?

Determined to keep her mind off her troubles, and maybe trim up those saddlebags, this afternoon she'd strolled along the powder-soft sand until she'd reached the island's unpopulated southern tip. Collecting shells and other flux, she'd happened upon a tree fallen across the full width of the beach. Its trunk had looked solid enough, but as she'd leaped over, her foot had broken through a patch of rotting wood. Off balance, she'd tumbled back, and had struck her head on something hard.

Nina touched that stinging lump now, and winced at the same time as another vivid memory flashed to mind.

A heartbeat before passing out she'd seen an angel standing on a nearby cliff…a brilliant vision, arched against the unsettled sky, which had made her heart hammer as well as melt.

She pushed up onto her elbows and angled her throbbing head. Tropical sunshine struggled through darkening clouds to bounce off the jagged ledges, but no angel adorned the cliff's peak.

Pity. The image burned into her brain was of a male

with raven's wing hair, linebacker shoulders and a set of windblown white wings. Given the distance, those few delicious details ought to have been it. And yet a deeper, unshakable impression remained…

Strong, chiselled features. Mesmerising ice-blue eyes. A bare chest bronzed the colour of warm oak. His confident stance had conveyed not only a sense of authority but also…

What was it?

Destiny? Perhaps purpose? And what about the raw sexuality that had rippled off him in blistering waves? Did angels have dibs on that stuff? She'd never seen anything more powerful.

More beautiful.

Before she'd slipped into darkness Nina imagined their eyes had met and a message had passed between them. He'd told her not to worry, that he knew and would protect her.

She looked around, and a slightly hysterical laugh slipped out.

How wild was that? And how fitting. These past months she'd needed a guardian angel and, with another enormous breaker rolling in, never more than now.

The rush of cool water flooded in, higher this time. As the wash ebbed out Nina tried to rotate her trapped ankle, but bit her lip when splinters pierced the skin. She tried sitting up to pry the wood away, but while the area her foot had penetrated was weak, the surrounding timber felt like concrete.

Slumping back, she covered her face with both wet, gritty hands and prayed.

Before her father had died her brother had also passed away, in tragic circumstances. Now her mother, her sister Jill and nephew Codie were the only family

Nina had left. She would give anything—*everything*—to get out of this and get back home to see them all again.

Another wave smashed on the sand. Frothy scallops swirled up, and this time Nina barely held her chin above water. Jill had always said her sister's one big flaw was her reluctance to accept help. Nina only wished Jill were here now. She wouldn't merely accept help, she'd happily beg. That roller about to break looked big enough to drown.

Assessing the dense grey-green foliage behind her, she waited for the cackle of a kookaburra to fade. Then she filled her lungs and, giving it her all, cried out—

"*Heeeelp!* Can anyone hear me? I need help!"

Long before Gabriel Steele heard the distant cry for help, he was hyper-aware of three things.

A: the thousand branches lashing at his flesh as he tore down the slope hurt like a bitch.

B: his new track shoes were worth their weight in gold.

C: he was running out of time.

His heart belting against his ribs, Gabriel kept his eye on each footfall as he rushed to negotiate the rugged decline. Fast was good. Reaching the bottom in one piece was better. He'd be as useful to that woman as a tiger with no teeth if he broke his leg—or his neck.

And why, in high heaven, had she wandered so far from the resort complex anyway?

Standing atop that cliff earlier, contemplating its drop and the danger, he'd seen her advance along the beach—had watched, unconcerned initially, when she'd skipped across that log. As if the wood were paper, her foot had plunged straight through. She'd toppled back, and when her head had hit that rock he'd felt the *thwack* to his bones.

Out cold.

And, because things could always get worse, the tide was pushing in.

He could boast better than twenty-twenty, but a blind man could see the situation looked grim.

Now, with shirt-tails flapping behind him, Gabriel bounced down the same steep track he'd climbed half an hour earlier. So much for stealing time to face a challenge that, for once, had nothing to do with corporate tax law.

In truth, he loathed taking time out from his position as director of Steele Chartered Accountants. During his decade-long rise up the corporate ladder he'd accrued a sizeable fortune, but he still had a way to go before his personal worth equalled that of his more affluent clients. He'd worked too damn hard to slack off now—particularly after breaking a cardinal rule.

Never over-extend.

Four weeks ago he'd taken a huge gamble, investing nearly all his equity in a venture he felt to his bones would pay off. The business's solvency had dropped close to bankruptcy, but if he made every move the right one he knew he could not only turn the entity around, he would also make it the envy of every tycoon in Australasia.

Now was "make or break" time. There was zero room for sentimentality. Less room for weak links.

"Help. *Pleeease.* Help!"

Brought back, Gabriel upped his pace. When a surprise branch whipped his forehead, his roar of a curse rattled the treetops. Once he'd shaken off the stars, he pushed all the harder. He had to reach that woman in time. He'd do the same for anyone.

Wished he *could* have done the same—

He tamped down futile memories to concentrate on his task, on that woman…and on the not unpleasant sensation that had curled in his stomach as he'd watched her from his vantage point earlier.

She seemed somehow familiar, her hair a caramel-gold waterfall pouring down her back, her legs endless, shapely and tanned. Stooping to collect a shell here and there, she'd conveyed a grace that only fine breeding could assure.

And yet her cut-offs were ragged around her firm thighs, and her feet were bare. No Manolo Blahnik flats in sight. Not that those legs needed expensive accessories. He could have watched her toned calves flex all day as she'd sifted through the powder-fine sand and—

A boulder sprang up out of nowhere. Gabriel hurdled and landed safely at the same time as a notion struck.

That was why she seemed so familiar. Watching her in those cut-offs had reminded him of a long-ago childhood vacation by the sea, when he'd gone barefoot twenty-four-seven and his fishing rod hadn't left his hand. Aunt Faith had been a gem, providing her studious nephew with plenty to eat and lashings of love. Despite the tragic circumstances surrounding his mother's disappearance, from the age of four Gabriel had enjoyed a well-rounded, relatively hassle-free upbringing.

Then his best friend had died.

At last Gabriel tore through the last layer of brush and burst into the light. His lungs burning from lack of air, his body lathered in sweat, he spotted the woman twenty metres away. He dug deep to mine what remained of his strength, then sprinted as the spill from a colossal wave consumed her.

His gaze held the circling froth where she'd disappeared until, plunging into the wet cool, he found her and urged her head clear of the torrent. As her arms shot out, and she gasped and coughed, he summed up the dire situation. Her ankle was locked at an ugly angle. No telling if bones had been broken.

One arm supporting her shoulders, he cleaned the filigree of clinging hair from her face as she struggled to take in air. If he'd had time to dwell he'd have said she was beautiful, in a bedraggled, drenched kitten kind of way.

"Can you hear me?" he asked. "Are you all right?"

She grasped the top of her leg and found a grateful smile. "I am now. I'm just a little—" She flinched. "A little in pain."

As the wave sucked back out he laid her down, then manipulated his fingers between her ankle and the wood. It seemed her foot had slipped through a knot; sadly, the surrounding shell felt tough as nails. She wouldn't have been able to budge it even if she'd had the strength to try.

After a couple of tugs, attempting to weaken the wood, he was quietly worried. He inhaled, rallied determination, and gave another, more serious wrench. A small piece broke off, then a bit more. No screams of pain; she gave little more than a thankful shudder as he freed her foot a second before water swept up and their world became a muted, cold-rush blur.

Fully submerged, holding his breath, he relied on his sense of touch to scoop the woman up and heave them both clear of the churning pool. He trudged well out of tide range and, on a sparsely grassed knoll, laid her down. Any minute the steady pump of adrenaline would give way to the burn of muscle fatigue, but for now he'd keep moving.

How bad were her injuries?

As she worked to catch her breath, Gabriel knelt close and collected her ankle. No compound fractures. When he rode two fingers over the arch of her foot, her peach-polished toes flexed up. Cupping her heel with one hand, his other palm resting on her shin, he applied a token amount of pressure to test the ligament. When she didn't complain, he applied a bit more. She cringed, but didn't cry out.

Brave girl.

There were nasty scratches and welts that would ripen to bruises. She'd need an X-ray, and a day or two of rest, but—fingers crossed—in a month or so her ankle would look as good as new.

Searching for other wounds, his gaze travelled the length of her leg, and higher. But at a tug low in his gut—a kick of kindling heat—he averted his eyes and cleared his throat. Inviting as she looked—wet tee-shirt moulding to the swell of her breasts, nipples puckered beneath transparent white interlock—this was *so* not the time.

He swept sand into a slanting step with one hand and then, to help with the swelling, set her foot upon the "pillow." Finally falling back on his rump, he laid one forearm on a raised knee, dragged down a settling breath, then blew it out in a rush. His heart was chugging like a steam train. He hadn't felt this juiced in years—not since torturing himself competing in triathlons in his late teens. Great for building stamina. Not so good for fending off ghosts.

He told her, "Nothing appears to be broken." *Thank God.*

Her chest deflated as she wheezed out a breath. "You sure? Coz it really isn't my day."

He grinned at her impish tone, her slight but sexy lisp. "You're scratched up, and—"

"My God—" Her eyes went wide in horror. "So are you."

As if to prove her point, a warm trickle slid past the corner of his eye. He ran his thumb over his temple, inspected the smear of blood, then swiped the red on his soaked chinos.

No headache. No sting. "Nothing serious."

Her unconvinced gaze zigzagged over his scored torso. "That's a whole pile of 'nothing serious,' if you ask me."

Her concern was appreciated, but he'd live. Thankfully so would she.

"There doesn't appear to be any ligament damage."

"Are you a doctor?"

"An accountant."

She looked uneasy. "No offence, but I thought accountants were supposed to wear black-rimmed glasses and look kind of nerdy."

He smiled. "No offence taken."

He'd worn just that type of glasses once—not that she needed to know. They were strangers, thrown together by situation and sheer luck. Of course that didn't mean they couldn't get to know one another. Might be the extraordinary circumstances, the overload of adrenaline, but somehow she seemed...

Different.

Oh, he dated. Hard not to when he was considered one of the country's most eligible bachelors, and friends constantly set him up with "possibilities." And, sure, women were nice. Hell, he wouldn't want to live in a world without them. But he was way too busy to worry about relationships. Too busy for anything other than casual.

As if that thought were a wish, an alternative vision of this woman swam up in his mind. With the tee removed, shortie-shorts too, her tan would be all over, her breasts mouth-wateringly full. The vee at the apex of her thighs shone with a tantalising tuft of caramel-gold—and *why,* dear heaven, was he letting his imagination run away on him like this?

Gabriel scrubbed his bristled jaw and shook his head clear.

Okay. Cold showers—and/or oceans—weren't cutting it any more. It had been way too long. Still, he could control his overloaded testosterone levels. Willpower, in everything, was his speciality.

He squared his shoulders, then moved to check the contusion on her head. After parting the clotted hair, his fingertips circled the injury and she hissed.

"Sorry," he murmured, then, "No cut. But you've got an egg."

"Laid by an emu, feels like."

Cupping her chin, he checked for uneven dilation of the pupils. When her large jewelled eyes blinked up at him, his groin flexed. Clearing his throat, he reminded himself of their circumstances and edged away.

"You were knocked out. Do you remember how it happened? Your name? Is there any ringing in your ears?"

What were the other signs of concussion?

But she didn't appear to be listening. Rather, those sparkling topaz eyes, surrounded by lush damp lashes, were examining him with new, almost innocent wonder.

"You were standing up there, weren't you? On that cliff."

His brows jumped. "You saw me?"

"Only for a moment." Her gaze dropped before catching his again. "This'll sound crazy, but as I blacked out I thought you were… Well, I thought you were an angel."

He chuckled at her almost reverent tone. "Sorry to disappoint you again." Not a doctor. Definitely not an angel.

As a late afternoon breeze rustled through the palm fronds, and seagulls squawked overhead, her eyes glistened and her brow furrowed more.

"Still, you…you seem familiar."

Really?

Maybe it was more than seaside memories that made her seem familiar too. Had they met before? At a dinner? Maybe they lived in the same neighbourhood? Potts Point, Sydney, was pricey, but then anyone vacationing at Diamond Shores had money and plenty of it.

Before he could ask, she held her head and groaned over an apologetic smile.

"I'm all muddled. My head feels like it's packed with cotton wool."

"I'm not surprised."

She needed that knock checked out properly, along with some painkillers and an appropriate bandage for her foot. She needed civilisation, asap.

"Give me a moment," he said, determined to ignore the creak of tightening hamstrings, "and I'll get you to a doctor."

The island enjoyed a full-time physician, as well as a seaplane and an emergency helicopter, both of which, he believed, served French champagne. Luxury at its decadent best.

"That'd be great," she said, tipping up. "You can lend me an arm. Or I could use a branch for a crutch."

He urged her back down. She needed to rest and lie flat. "You're not walking anywhere."

Her doubtful gaze drilled his. "What'll we do, then? Close our eyes and click our heels three times?"

He grinned. Cute.

"I'll carry you."

"All the way to the resort?" She half coughed, half laughed. "Your arms will break off."

He cocked a brow. "I assure you they won't."

Her cheeks pinked up before she gave a conciliatory sigh. "Look, I appreciate everything you've done. You've been two hundred percent chivalrous and I'll be forever grateful. But I'm not exactly a flyweight."

Correct. She was shapely. Voluptuous, really. Precisely how a woman ought to be.

He cut short his discreet assessment at the same time as she pushed back up on her elbows and sent over an all-settled, I'm-used-to-getting-my-own-way smile. "So, we're agreed?"

His hand on her shoulder eased her down again. "Lie flat." She didn't need to risk nausea or dizziness. "I'll do whatever needs to be done."

"That can't include giving yourself a heart attack." Her eyes lit up. "I know. You can go for help and I'll wait here."

"You need medical attention now, not later."

Besides, he wouldn't leave her alone. She might get it into her head that she knew best and try to limp back to the resort.

"You don't understand," she said. "I was big-boned before getting friendly with the food here. If you've tried the desserts, you'll know you can't stop at one."

Her lush lips were soft and parted now, and a delicate pulse beat at the base of her throat. I wonder what that pulse would feel like against my tongue? Gabriel thought.

Wonder what she'd be like in bed?

"Hello?" she cooed. "Are you listening?"

He grunted, drove a hand through his hair. "Sure. Delicious. No control."

She nodded, then winced and touched her head. "You're all fired up, and obviously capable, but I can't have you putting your back out." She pushed up again. "And, seeing I have final say in the matter—"

"Absolutely you have a say." He tipped her back down. "You can say, *Yes, sir.*"

Her mouth dropped open and a mew of outrage escaped.

Doubly determined, she pushed up again. "I didn't realise I'd joined the army."

"I'll count to three," he warned, half hoping she'd defy him.

She didn't disappoint. "I'm more than capable of making my own decisions, thank you very much."

Done with words, he pointed at the ground. When her face hardened with a you-can't-make-me look, his jaw shifted. He admired spunk, but only one person was in charge here and it was time she learned who that was.

In one smooth, purposeful movement, he angled closer, crowding her back as he bent forward until, eyes gone wide, she lay horizontal again. By the time he stopped crowding, his head was slanted over hers and their mouths all but touched.

His gaze licked her lips as he grinned.

"You were saying?"

CHAPTER TWO

STARING into the wicked eyes of a beast, Nina kept still and swallowed hard.

There she'd been, wondering if she could possibly get out of that fix alive, then *pow!* So broad through the chest, so capable and infuriatingly confident, this superhero type showed up out of nowhere.

But she was confused. Where did he fit on her character chart? Was this man exceptionally good, or primarily perfectly bad?

Anyone with half a brain and a pair of scales must see he couldn't carry her all the way back to the resort. Nevertheless, he hadn't merely dismissed her suggestions. He'd gone so far as to pin her body beneath his to get his point across.

She was trapped. She should be fuming!

Instead her nerve-endings simmered with indisputable awareness, and her fuzzy brain kept wondering how well his lips might fit closed over hers.

"You're quiet," he noted, his mouth a hair's breadth from hers.

Wondering if he might manacle her wrists next—and not wholly against the idea—she squirmed. "I'm thinking."

"About behaving, I hope."

His voice was rough, dangerously deep, and the whisper of his breath against her lips felt far less invasive than it ought to.

"Do I need to point out," she said, "that I'm not the one behaving badly?"

"Won't make a difference. If I let you have your way, you could do yourself another injury." Wet dark hair flopped over his brow when he cocked his head. "Or would you rather I ignore the fact you might have concussion?"

"I'd rather you quit with the caveman mentality."

He growled and leaned a smidge closer. "You're only alive because that caveman mentality got me to you before the sharks tucked in for dinner."

She held her breath while her heart thumped high in her chest.

Oh, crap. She hated to admit it, but his brutish logic made sense. He would never convince her he could carry her all the way back to the resort, but her head did feel light. If she stood up now, tried to walk, she might very well fall over. Maybe even knock herself out a second time. Like it or not, in a roughish kind of way, he was still rescuing her—protecting her—this time from herself.

She issued a reluctant nod and, fire fading from his eyes, he curled away.

As he repositioned himself beside her, the sinking sun fell behind his head, bathing his splendid form in a golden-rose halo. Nina squeezed her eyes shut, then looked again. He wasn't an angel. She was certain of that now. And yet his presence, this scene, everything about this time here with him seemed surreal. Make-believe.

Maybe she was still unconscious? Maybe her lungs were filled with water and she'd hallucinated all this while succumbing to the final phase of drowning? Was she experiencing some incredible dream on her way to the hereafter? That wasn't so unlikely. She'd heard stories before.

Was any of this real?

Determined to find out, she reached and touched his pec, an inch above that small flat nipple. Her fingertip sizzled like creamy butter on a hotplate, at the same time as her centre glowed and blood tingled with fresh life. As her fingers fanned over the black, crisp hair, bolts of crackling electricity ripped through her veins. His flesh was so firm, so masculine and—

She stopped.

Inched her gaze up.

He was looking down his aquiline nose at her fingers—which were kneading the warm cushioned steel as if they belonged there.

Tilting his cleft chin, he raised a dark brow and his entrancing eyes met hers.

"Let me know when it's my turn."

She snatched her hand away. Her breathing was all over the place again and her face was flaming. Simply put, she wanted to die.

"I was just…er…just making sure they were—I mean, that *you* were—" Embarrassed beyond words, she spat out the rest. "I was making sure you were real."

"Oh, is *that* what you were doing?"

His lopsided grin drew a crease down one side of that highly kissable mouth. And his eyes…

They were so clear and bright and *laughing*.

Laughing at her.

She understood why. She was acting like a loon. A suspicious, ungrateful, concussed, groping loon.

But then his gaze sharpened and his expression changed.

"Are you cold?" he asked, edging close again.

"I don't think so." But that noise… Were her teeth chattering? Checking out the clouds building to black overhead, she shivered and instinctively hugged herself. "I am kind of shaky."

A line cut between his brows and he cupped her chin, turned her head gently one way then the next. His gaze intensified, and for a giddy moment Nina imagined she'd fallen head-first into those amazing ice-blue eyes. When he checked her pulse against his platinum Omega, she relented and played compliant patient. After six weeks of serving other people's every whim, there was part of her that needed this one-on-one attention, mandatory though the attention might be.

"What's the verdict, Doc?" Did he want her to open her mouth and say *ah?*

Her answer came when he rolled his shoulders back and peeled off his shirt. Her eyes popped out of her head. *Mamma mia.* What a specimen.

"You need to be kept warm," he told her, stripping a sleeve off one dynamite arm and then the other.

"Thanks," she managed to wheeze, "but I don't think a wet shirt will cut it."

"Body heat will."

"Y-you're going to *hold* me?"

He blindly tossed the shirt on a bush, then loomed over her, the chiselled planes of his face unforgivably close. "Any objection?"

Her gaze zeroed in on his mouth, on the dusky pink of his full bottom lip, and her pelvic floor muscles squeezed.

She'd tried to refuse him before and her opposition

had got her nowhere. If anything, being obstinate had made matters worse. An air of entitlement, albeit tempered by *GQ* looks and bad-boy charm, was a quality that stuck in her craw. She'd kow-towed to similar sorts too often these past weeks…people who would once have classed her as their equal.

All that aside, this guy was no idiot. If he said she needed to be held—hell, he was probably right. And if she must be gathered up against some unknown body… heck, it might as well be his.

When she mustered a haughty look and shrugged one shoulder, he scooped an arm beneath her neck.

"Tell me if I hurt you," he said, careful of her bump and her foot as he lay beside her.

He drew her close until her ear rested on the plateau of flesh and muscle below his collarbone. Despite her irritation, she almost sighed when one iron-warm palm splayed over the small of her back, pressing her deftly against his powerhouse length.

His breath brushed her ear. "How's that?"

She could be smarmy, could fib and say she was uncomfortable; she *was* in a way—only because he had, indeed, been right. It seemed those remarkable arms gathering her near were exactly what her traumatised body had needed.

Comfort…a masculine mountain of it.

She buried her nose in his chest and mumbled, "Better."

She imagined his grin. "Good."

He was damp but hot, as if a furnace were blazing away beneath the skin, and when she closed her eyes everything but the impression of security and strength faded from mind. His earthy scent, mixed with a lingering hint of aftershave or soap, burrowed into her pores and played havoc with her rag-taggle reason.

This felt nice. *He* felt nice. Nice and strong and not-so-plain-or-simple sexy.

She inwardly sighed.

Oh, why not admit it? The throb in the base of her belly wasn't a consequence of relief or gratitude, or even exasperation. It was desire—the forbidden, molten lava kind that blocked out other stimuli, heightened each sense and alerted every fibre. It was the kind of intense physical attraction that had her half convinced she needed to dissolve into this man right here, right now, or simply cease to be.

Crazy.

Clearly the knock on her head had bumped the arousal lever in her brain up to high. Every synapse seemed to have direct dial to the pulse ticking merrily away between her thighs. Every nerve-ending was wired to zap the burning tips of her breasts. All of which made her horribly nervous.

And terribly curious.

They were strangers, brought together by near tragedy. She was a level-headed woman who, admittedly, hadn't had a man in a while. A good while. And certainly never one like *this*. But her urge to gaze up, look into those incredible eyes and offer him her lips…

It was wrong. Totally off beam.

Wasn't it?

A moment ago his bedraggled kitten had wanted to know if this was real. Now Gabriel wondered too. He hadn't peeled off his shirt and drawn her close for any reason other than her shaking. She needed to be kept warm.

Sure, he was benefiting too. Lying on this cushiony spread of sandy grass and listening to the rhythmic wash of waves gave him a chance to recuperate. His system needed a break. Only…

He didn't feel all that relaxed.

His body was a simmering mass of anticipation. His heartbeat was a booming bass beat in his ears. Those symptoms weren't a consequence of exertion any more than the ambitious tightening in his groin, or the groan of awareness building like thermal movement deep in his chest.

He was a man who lived well—the finest food and accommodation, state-of-the-art high-powered cars. But holding a beautiful woman was on a shelf all its own. *She* seemed to be on a shelf all her own.

He was no stranger to sex. Slow sex, hot sex—wild sex even better. But, no matter how stimulating the company, he'd never needed to worry about maintaining a certain level of control. He never truly lost himself in the moment. And yet the desire rippling through his veins now was distinct. Unique.

Disturbing.

It had to be the setting, the extraordinary circumstances, but it was all he could do not to tug this woman's supple curves closer, coax her shapely hips nearer, tilt her chin higher and kiss her.

Hard.

Normally he knew when a woman was interested too. A lidded look. An arched brow. A sensual smile when she caught his gaze and held it. That kind of nonverbal communication had been perfected by nature over eons to ensure the survival of the species. *I'm available. Me too.* No genius there.

But, lying beneath this palm tree with Miz Crusoe nestled alongside him, he was stumped. She'd been grateful, stubborn, teasing, and finally accepting. It couldn't be his imagination that she was enjoying this contact as much as he was.

So where did pumped-up high-stakes drama end, and good old-fashioned foreplay with an attractive, might-as-well-be-naked woman begin? If he rolled more towards her, how would she react? With outrage, as she'd done earlier, before he'd flattened her against the ground to make sure she wouldn't hurt herself? Or would her gaze become heavy with an I-feel-it-too glow?

When she gave a violent shiver, the choice was made for him. Before she trembled a second time Gabriel held her more firmly, grazing a warming palm up and down her chilled arm.

After a moment she looked up, and her full lips twitched. "You must think I'm horrible."

He grinned. "Worse than Godzilla and the giant Powder Puff man combined."

Her perfect smile fanned wider before she sobered. "While I can't condone all your tactics, I truly am grateful. For everything. You're right. I'd have been fish food if you hadn't come along when you did."

"I'm glad I was able to help." More than she'd ever know. "How's your foot?"

Her leg moved and she flinched. "Hurts a little."

"We ought to get moving before the pain gets worse."

She hummed out an affirmation, but then only laid her cheek back upon his chest.

He gauged the sun's heavy position in the sky, the storm clouds meshing together overhead, then closed his eyes and concentrated on the feel of her hand on his ribs.

Ah, what the hell? A few more minutes wouldn't hurt.

His palm trailed her arm again, up over the slender shoulder, down to her elbow. Seagulls wheeled and squawked above while time wrapped around them like a promise-filled cocoon. If anyone had happened along they'd have mistaken them for lovers.

"Guess we really should get going," she murmured. "You've probably got someone waiting."

He nailed the quality in her voice: overly blasé. People came to Diamond Shores to fulfil their island fantasy while soaking up every laid-back luxury. Make the rates exorbitant, and it was a licence to print money. It added up that kitten here was looking to be indulged too. But in what way? And to what extent?

Time for a test line.

"There's nobody waiting in the way you're implying," he said.

"What way is that?"

"How many ways are there?"

"Let's see. You could be here on a reckless weekend with a bud."

"Nope."

"Could be showing a client a good time, hoping to tie the bow on a multi-million-dollar deal."

"Good guess, but no banana."

"You're here with your girl?"

"Don't have one."

Two beats of silence, then her breath brushed his chest again. "Maybe you're here to find one?"

"Is that an invitation?"

She gave a humourless laugh, but didn't search out his gaze. "Believe me, I'm not your type."

"What type are you?"

"I should start with clumsy."

"So this kind of incident isn't a one-off?"

"Yesterday I spilled a drink in the lap of an Arab prince."

He cringed. "Bet he offered to buy you another one."

When she groaned, the vibration blew a pleasant tingling rash down one side of his body. "Hardly."

"International model types weren't the Prince's thing?"

She lifted her head to give him a pull-the-other-one look. "Models are super tall and thin."

"So, not a model?" he conjectured. "More athlete, then. You compete in the European show-jump circuit?"

"Horses make me sneeze. And I'm clumsy, remember? I'd break my neck, and the poor horse's too."

"Okay. Your father's one of the country's leading barristers and you're fresh out of law school, ready to fry your first bad guy's butt," he surmised, and she laughed.

"I like your imagination," she said, "but…"

"I'm off track?"

"Way off."

"A hint would be good."

"But not as fun as hearing what you come up with next."

Her eyes were dancing now, and a stream of hair had fallen down the centre of her forehead, criss-crossing her slim straight nose. He scooped the hair behind her ear and his blood heated more.

"Got it." He lowered his hand. "You're a misunderstood heiress running from the press."

"Not this year."

He chuckled, so she did too, but then she winced and touched her head.

His stomach muscles crunched and welts stung for the first time as he sat up. "How's the lump?"

"Only hurts when I laugh."

He mock-frowned. "I can be serious."

"Tell me something I don't know."

"I want to hold you closer."

Her hand drifted away from her bump. "You want to do what?"

"Hold you closer."

Her eyes rounded to saucers.

"That's not a command, by the way," he added. "More a suggestion."

"If I say no?"

"We head off to the resort."

"If I say yes?"

"Then I'll add another wish to my list."

She blinked several times, as if she were having trouble taking it all in, but she didn't try to wriggle away. In fact she leaned nearer. "Tell me."

He craned his neck to graze his lips over the satin and grit of her brow, and the contact made the skin tighten over his flesh. "I'd do this."

He heard her intake of air, felt her slight tremble as he grazed again.

Her hand bunched slowly on his chest, sending positive signals to regions below.

"And then?" she asked.

He cupped her nape, his thumb circling the base of her neck before his hand slid around to her chin. His lips skied down the slope where a moment ago he'd brushed her hair away.

"I'd tip your chin higher." With a knuckle, he angled her mouth towards his. "Like this."

Her lips parted as she inhaled, silent but deep, and her heavy gaze sparkled into his.

"Then what?"

Smiling softly, he moved closer.

"Then this."

CHAPTER THREE

THE touch of his kiss was faint, yet the intensity of sensation was all-consuming. The promise of what was to come gave Nina a heady rush and goosebumps down to her toes. Today she'd nearly lost her life, but this—dear heaven—was almost worth dying for.

With his thumb guiding her jaw, he steered her chin higher and kissed her again, this time with his mouth slanted at a different, more exacting angle.

Nina sighed.

He felt like magic…omnipotent, skilled, sultry. This caress was barely there, yet somehow it lifted her to another plane, where warm hands understood how to stroke and leisurely lips knew how to thrill. If there was an advanced school of kissing, this guy had graduated top of the class.

As his mouth reluctantly drew away, the tip of his nose brushed hers. She opened her eyes, and when he opened his, they were a dark, stormy blue-grey, and filled with a latent hunger Nina's surging blood recognised too.

This man was every woman's dream. Masterful, challenging, sexy to a fault. She'd never met anyone like him. She wanted him to kiss her a second time, and then she wanted him to do it again.

One problem.

Did she tell him before or after she wasn't who or what he thought? Not an heiress fleeing from the paparazzi, not the genius daughter of a world-famous barrister, but a rather average, stressed-out waitress, struggling to get through a difficult time.

Good thing he had track shoes on. He might want to run a mile.

"I have to say," he murmured in a rich, drugging voice that spoke directly to her G spot, "that felt good."

Despite her concerns, she couldn't help but smile back. "I second that."

His absorbed gaze dropped to devour her lips. "I vote we get more inventive."

"Which entails…?"

"For you…simply lie back and enjoy."

"Oh, I have to *enjoy* it?" she teased.

He nipped her bottom lip. "That's the idea."

At the notion of total surrender—arms draped over her head, taking every wonderful delight he had to offer—syrupy warmth condensed at the heart of her. The idea of making love with a thoroughly gorgeous man she barely knew was not only reckless, it was irresistible. Who said she wasn't allowed to forget her problems for an hour or two? Wrapping herself in his silver lining sounded pretty good about now.

With a cooling breeze blowing over her skin, teasing her nipples, she wet her lips.

"What about you? Do you get to enjoy it too?"

He shifted up, so that one side of his impressive chest hovered over hers. His arm curled possessively above her head.

"Ask me a hard question."

He kissed her in earnest then, his warmth flashing

heat-lightning through her blood, his mouth irrevocably claiming hers. But not in a gulping, feverish fashion. More with the finesse of a man who knew what women liked. What *this* woman needed.

His slightly roughened palm trailed down her neck. His thumb rested in the hollow of her beating throat before his touch skimmed down her décolletage, then slid to encircle her upper arm, coaxing her up and in. The suggestion of ownership in the gesture was unmistakable, as well as enthralling—all the more so given the way his mouth worked unhurriedly yet intently with hers.

Her arms coiled around his neck and she pulled herself up, offering more, as delectable desire built and bubbled away—a steaming kettle ready to boil. She was physically, helplessly drawn to him, like a tide to the moon or a bird to blue sky. When his tongue probed deeper Nina whimpered with mind-tingling longing, and a strange sense of belonging seeped through her.

This embrace wasn't merely great, it was fated. In this thin slice of time she wasn't Jill's sister or little Codie's aunt. She wasn't the pampered princess who'd once had everything, or the twenty-year-old who'd slogged her guts out to ace her journalism class. She wasn't a magazine editor who'd found herself at a crossroads.

At this moment she was pure woman, hovering at the pinnacle of creation's best ever kiss. She felt so fired up she could barely breathe—but, unlike during her near drowning moments ago, she didn't want to come up for air. She'd much rather relinquish herself to her mystery man's caress until she expired from exhaustion and sheer joy.

When his thumb brushed the outside of her breast

she groaned. The sensitive peak tightened and her leg instinctively moved in. But the scratches on her ankle rubbed and, wincing, she jerked back an inch. When he pulled back too, the set of his jaw and refocusing eyes said he'd remembered where they were.

Oh, but this couldn't end now. What were a couple of scratches compared to the chance to truly escape and float on cloud nine?

Her arm still around his neck, she tugged. "I'm perfectly fine—honest."

His chin kicked up a notch. "You don't know how much I'd like to believe that."

Her fingers filed up through the back of his hair. "Believe it."

He set his forehead upon hers. "I'm afraid this, my dear, is not the time."

She pouted. "Really?"

"*Really,* really."

Sorry. She couldn't accept it. Her hand snaked down and she drew a suggestive circle around his right nipple, smiling when the disc hardened beneath her touch.

Folding her hand up in his, he pressed his warm lips to the palm. "Doctor first. Advanced introductions later."

"Maybe one more quick hello?"

He laughed, a gorgeous black velvet sound she would never tire of hearing. This guy had it all. Looks, charm, Herculean strength. Sure, he was a little over-confident, but, given the circumstances, after that kiss, she could find it in her heart to forgive him.

"Later," he confirmed, and cocked an enquiring brow. "Maybe over dinner?"

Nina's expression dissolved into a walking-on-air smile.

Fate was so unpredictable. A couple of months ago she'd had the next ten years mapped out—work her way up the magazine industry ladder and ultimately secure a spot on a top international rag overseas. By that time Jill would have met the guy of her dreams and Codie would be a real little man. One day Nina had hoped to find her soul mate—someone who truly understood and respected her.

Then her life had landed in a dumpster.

From heiress to editor to wayward waitress. What came next?

When her Galahad sprang to his feet and dusted himself off, Nina sighed. The most amazing few minutes of her life were over. But there was always dinner tonight.

Or was there?

The clientele here seemed oblivious to everything other than their own over-inflated issues and comfort. They lived to compare carats over a leisurely back rub or two. Was this man cut from that same cloth? How would he react when he found out he'd been making love to the hired help?

And, if that wasn't enough to dampen those dinner plans, there was always the resort's staunchest staff rule. No socialising with guests. *Ever.*

His shadow crept over her a second before his strong arms scooped beneath her shoulders and knees. Jolted back, she pushed against his chest. "What are you doing?"

"We've had this discussion."

"I'm not sure we came to any decision." None that she'd been happy with.

"If memory serves, you called me a caveman, I beat my chest, and the matter was settled. Now, we need to hurry. Rain's on the way."

Folding her arms over her waist, she tried to weigh herself down—not that she wasn't heavy enough. Nevertheless, he swooped her effortlessly up.

His white teeth flashed. "Light as a feather."

Uh-huh? Veins were already popping at his temples. She could sense the strain in his arms. Why-oh-why had she taken that slab of chocolate torte back to her room last night?

"Put your arms around my neck," he ordered.

"So you're intent on doing this?" *Giving yourself a hernia.*

His response was a sexy wry smile.

She held his gaze, then finally exhaled. He was implacable. What choice did she have? She only hoped he didn't keel over from a coronary before he'd finished saving her.

She was securing her arms around his hot neck when a light bulb went off in her head. "Hey, I've had another thought. You could make a tray out of a big banana leaf and pull me along. Like a snow sled, only on sand."

His eyes narrowed even as he smiled. "No bananas growing here."

"Well, you must have a cellphone. You could call for the helicopter to chopper me out. We could make a giant X on the beach with driftwood so they know where to land, and—"

Her words were cut off when his mouth took hers. And just like that the magic was in full swing again, drifting over her like tingling confetti as his kiss worked its spell and he urged her against his granite-like frame.

She dissolved into him. Melted completely. Of its own volition a hand wandered to the centre of his hard chest, fanned over the rock of a pec, then sailed higher, tracking the topography of the bulging cords in his neck, the sandpaper bristle of his firm square jaw. Only when his mouth left hers did the fog partly lift and she realised.

It was sprinkling rain.

Lifting her face, Nina blinked as another drop hit her cheek, then her arm. When he looked up too, as if waving a green flag, the rain came down in earnest.

She let go a shriek. Could her poor body take another beating?

But, while the rain fell in buckets, the water felt soft and revitalising on her skin. Perhaps it was her near brush with death, the lingering effects of that better-than-bliss kiss, or the fact that for the first time in weeks she felt truly free, but a jet of abandon surged up from her centre and a bubble of laughter escaped. Going with impulse, she shut her eyes and tilted back her head. When she opened her mouth wide, sweet rain filled her throat.

She gulped twice, three times, then, through the gauzy mist of rain, searched out his eyes.

Streams were coursing down his ruggedly handsome face, running off the tip of his nose. He studied her, his head slanted, before a crooked smile broke and he rocked back his neck as she had done. Laughing again, she joined him, and as he held her beneath the opened sky, she felt their strength restored.

Some quenching moments later he shook his head, like a dog after a bath, then near shouted over the water clattering through the layers of thirsty foliage behind them.

"We need shelter."

From beneath sodden lashes, she cast a glance around. The sea had darkened and whipped up too, each slate-green crest rising ever higher before smashing on the shore. The evocative scent of fresh rainfall seemed to rise off the earth's every pore. No birds in the sky, no tiny soldier crabs scurrying over the sand…everything seemed hidden away, as if nature had called a time out.

As the rain fell harder still, he took matters into his own hands—but he didn't charge north towards the resort. Rather he headed inland, weaving with precise guerrilla-like movements through a break in the bush.

"Cover your face," he called as he strode through the underbrush.

She did as he asked and protected herself. "Where are we going?"

Was there a cave close by?

But he didn't answer, and she didn't push. Curling into him, making herself small against the branches lashing by, once again she put her faith in this remarkable man.

Finally his gait slowed, and she was jolted when his shoulder crashed against something hard. Then the rain stopped, although she still heard it…

Thrashing on a roof?

Gingerly she uncovered her face and swiped sopping hair from her eyes, in time to see him kick a crude-looking door shut. The noise of the rain outside was cut off and they were alone, dripping puddles at the inside entrance of what looked to be a cabin—boxy, barely furnished, and located in the middle of the island's dense tropical forest.

He crossed to a single wooden chair set beside a small round table. In the shadowy light she saw a coffee cup pushed near the plastered wall. When he lowered her upon the chair her arm unravelled from around his neck, and as his warmth drew away a violent chill racked her body. She hugged herself as he moved to a kitchenette and flicked a switch. Over the din on the tin roof, her ears picked up the hiss of a kettle.

She twined her legs around one another and, hunching her shoulders, rubbed the gooseflesh on her arms. The exposed beam ceiling was low. An old sepia-tone photo hung on the opposite wall. A gnarly wooden coatstand guarded the door. The only other furniture was a double bed to her right. Shivering, Nina clutched herself tighter. That plump blue and yellow patchwork quilt looked mighty inviting.

The photo on the wall drew her eye. A gently smiling woman sat sloped towards her husband. Humour shone in the man's dark eyes, and Nina almost felt his hand lying upon her shoulder, as it did on his wife's in the picture. The hairstyles and garb said mid last-century.

"How did you find this place?" she asked. Had he stumbled upon it during his walk?

The kettle had boiled and he was sliding a coffee bottle over the counter. It was overly large, with a palm tree embossed on one side. It must have been here as long as that picture.

"This isn't what you're used to, I expect."

An unpolished wooden floor, a square-paned window with no curtain to draw against a view of the deluge. The cabin was austere, but also dry and cosy… and, in its intimate isolation, rustically romantic. But foremost it was somebody else's property. Were the people in that photo still alive? Given the circumstances, she supposed the owners wouldn't mind them sheltering here, but she frowned as he poured water from the kettle.

"Do you think we should help ourselves to the pantry?"

He paused, setting the kettle down, but then sent

over a smile. "This place is mine for the week—along with a bungalow back at the resort."

Nina lifted her brows. So this millionaire liked to rough it? And this was about as rough as it got.

He asked about sugar and milk. It seemed they both liked their coffee black, so he added some cold water from the tap and brought the much appreciated drink over.

Taking the warm mug in two hands, she sipped. The bitter but tasty brew filtered heat through her blood and most of the goosebumps faded.

Running an eye over the kitchen—retro orange tiles, super-old stove, modern microwave—she pressed the mug to her cheek, then her breastbone. "How did you know this even existed?" She hadn't heard a murmur about a rental bush cabin from the staff.

He heeled off his shoes near the cold ashes of the fireplace. "The owner built it decades ago." She had her mouth open to ask more, but he changed the subject. "You need to get out of those clothes."

The nerves high in Nina's stomach kicked—firstly at his words, then at the thought of that double bed and its come-hither quilt. But he wasn't suggesting anything other than the obvious. The rain had set in, and sitting here, shivering and sopping, wasn't smart. They both needed to get dry.

Striding past her towards the bed, he threw back a filmy curtain, which was hooked up to a chrome rail. "I'll run a tub and you can get that grit off."

Nina craned her neck. A chipped porcelain clawfoot bathtub. Hardly five-star—she set her mug aside—but if hot water was involved, she was there.

After he had twisted the stiff faucets, unseen pipes shuddered and groaned to life. He tested the water and, with the other hand propping his weight on the tub's rim, sought out her gaze.

"You okay to undress and get in?"

His question came at the same time as she found her feet. Her blood pressure dropped and, suddenly giddy, she closed her eyes and withered back down.

He was concerned she mightn't be able to manage with her ankle, but for her this last half-hour had moved too fast. First the appearance of her angel on the cliff, then the rescue, heightened by that once-in-a-lifetime kiss. Finally she'd been whisked away to this delectable man's secret lair.

On the beach, as his hands had traced over her body and his mouth had covered hers, she'd craved far more than his kiss. Here was her opportunity. Maybe she ought to take up his offer to help her undress.

She felt a familiar heat and opened her eyes. He was hunkered down beside her, dark brows drawn, the bristles on his jaw rough and close enough to touch.

"Hey…you all right?"

Genuine concern shone in his eyes. For so many reasons, it wasn't the time to think beyond what was relevant. Salt had dried on her skin where the rain hadn't reached. Sand, stuck to her shorts and her back, rubbed against the seat. And her scratches should be washed out properly too. Never mind about getting naked. Right now she needed to get clean.

Carefully she pushed to her feet again. "I think a hot bath is exactly what I need."

He loaned her an arm, collected the chair in his free hand, and she hobbled with him over to the tub. He set the chair below a tarnished brass rack and, before drawing the curtain, said, "That's a fresh towel."

Then the curtain whizzed closed and she was alone.

She slipped out of her clothes. When a perfect fan-shaped shell fell from her shorts pocket she set it on a rickety shelf. A few minutes later she slipped into warm liquid heaven.

Her ankle twinged briefly before she slid against the porcelain until she was fully under. Working her fingertips over her skull and through her hair, she shifted the stubborn sand and salt. After coming up for air, she repeated the exercise twice more. Then she closed her eyes and, resting her neck against the rim, simply floated.

When her nostrils blew air into the water, she yanked herself up with a start. She'd drifted close to sleep, and the bath had lost its steamy edge. Past time to dry off.

But as she reached for the towel her attention honed in on the rain, still thumping on the roof, and the wet clothes piled near the chair.

Her throat closed.

She had nothing to wear.

A gust of wind blew the curtain in, and she snatched the towel to her breast. But the wind dropped just as suddenly as it had appeared and the curtain fell straight again.

Wet hair running rivers over her shoulders, Nina first straddled the bath's rim then, careful of her foot, stepped out and secured the towel under her arms. The door had opened and shut; her companion must have left while she'd been submerged, rinsing out her hair. But where had he gone?

Wondering if she should call out, she instead peeked around the curtain's corner—and her legs all but buckled.

CHAPTER FOUR

NINA'S face flamed and her toes dug into the floor. She'd enjoyed the sight of her half-naked angel earlier, but she had only imagined the full, delectable picture standing before her now.

His back to her, he stood in the middle of the room, saturated—including the towel he now unravelled from around his hips. The moving shadows of early evening had deepened on the walls, but nothing could dim the glistening outline of his broad back as he tossed the towel near the unlit fireplace, where it landed with a heavy *slap*.

Bands of sinew roped in his arm when he stretched to retrieve a second towel from the table, and when he tousle-dried his hair—his long legs braced apart—Nina couldn't tear her gaze from his hamstrings…thick and hard and rock-solid scrumptious. His buns were tight too, and beautifully masculine; she lost her breath each time he rubbed himself and one or the other flexed in turn. When he flicked the towel behind his head and gave his back a two-handed rub down, the rippling muscles sang to her like a Ravel composition come to life.

Too soon he knotted that towel around his hips and thrust both hands through his damp dark hair. At the same time he rotated her way. Her mind slotted into gear and Nina ducked back behind the curtain. Heartbeat knocking at her ribs, she watched his shadow's languid gait as he moved towards the bed. She bit her lip and almost whimpered. To think a man like that truly existed and, better yet, was here with her.

"Are you all right back there?"

At the deep enquiring voice Nina's pulse leapt and she squeaked, "Fine. I'm fine."

"I used the outside shower to wash off."

Outside shower? "Oh?"

"A broken drainpipe," he explained, at the same time as an arm materialised behind the curtain. A green chequered shirt was thrust towards her.

"This'll have to do for now," came the voice, so near and rich the vibrations shot a fiery dart directly at her core. "Can't help in the underwear department," he added as she took the shirt and the hand withdrew. "When you're dressed we'll bandage those cuts. I want to know they're clean."

She finished drying, then slipped the oversized laundered shirt over her head. *Bath, shirt, bandages. Do this, do that.* He might have saved her life, but did he ever give over being such a *boss?*

Shirt-tails brushing her knees, she straightened the collar, then drew back the curtain and said, "You love being in charge, don't you?"

He was crouched by a kitchen cupboard. He seemed to deliberate on his answer and then, hitching back one shoulder, pushed to his bare feet. "It's what I do."

Right. Like Alexander had led armies. Only Alexander hadn't been a bean-counter—

And he hadn't worn jeans like *this* man could.

But even as she unconsciously wet her lips at the

heart-pumping sight standing tall before her, another vision sprang to mind and she couldn't smother a laugh.

A wry glint in his eye, he sauntered over. "What's the joke?"

"It's just *commanding* and *accountant* don't seem to go. I can't help picturing a masked crusader, with a big A on his chest and a turbo-blasting calculator cocked in one hand."

Faint lines branching from the corners of his eyes deepened. "Never underestimate the power of a turbo-blasting calculator." His gaze fixed on hers, he moved closer still, the low band of his jeans riding and sliding with each deliberate step.

"What about you?"

"Me?" Her attention shot up from the dark hair trailing down from his navel. "What about me?"

"We're done with the guessing game. Spill." His pale eyes twinkled. "Who are you?"

Very good question.

"I'm…er…in hospitality."

His eyes darkened. "Here to check out the opposition?"

"I'm a hands-on type."

He nodded as if he understood. "How long are you staying?"

"That's up in the air."

Seemingly not surprised, he undid the first aid kit she now realised he held. "I'm here for a wedding on Saturday."

"The Wilson wedding?"

His gaze sharpened. "You're a friend of April's?"

"Not exactly."

"A friend of the groom's, then? I'm Gabriel Steele, by the way. April's boss. Or should I say former boss."

"The bride-to-be resigned?" she asked, and he nodded. "And you're not happy about it."

A muscle in his jaw jumped twice before he crossed to the fireplace. He placed the first aid kit on the mantel and, with kindling prepared, struck a match. "April's a great PA."

"Guess her fiancé thinks she'll make a great wife." And he didn't want to share with macho man here. Understandable. She'd bet Gabriel had a harem of Girl Fridays back at the office, all eager to rip their veils off.

He retrieved a poker and, with one perfectly sculptured arm bracing the mantel, stirred the embers while virgin flames licked around the logs. "These days I didn't think marriage meant a woman had to give up her career." He sniffed. "But good luck to them."

A vote for feminism? Nina thought not. Did he disapprove of his PA's fiancé? Or were his reasons more personal? Perhaps he had a thing for this April himself? Or was it more a classic case of "eligible male against marriage" syndrome? Those guys ought to form a club.

But then her mind scuttled back to his name.

She'd known a Gabriel once. Of course she hadn't seen or heard from him in years. Not since the funeral.

Her stomach double-clutched at the thought of that day and she studied her host's face again, this time in the wavering firelight. The hawkish nose, the cleft in his shadowed chin, the sharp widow's peak dead centre of his forehead as he set the poker aside.

The Gabriel she'd known—Gabe Turner—had been a friend of her brother's, and they'd made an unlikely pair. While Anthony had been sporty, charming, and much sought after by the girls, Geeky Gabe had sat on the chess squad, had worn his hair parted way over on one side, and had owned glasses with super-thick lenses that darkened when hit by the light. Sadder still, Gabe had been poor…or poor by Petrelle standards.

One day she'd let Gabe into their house—more like a three-storey mansion—and when he'd taken off his shoes at the front door, the fourteen-year-old Nina had been appalled. A hole in both sets of toes. She'd whispered across, asking whether they could perhaps buy him a new pair, but Gabe had pressed his lips together and, hands clenched, strode off to Anthony's room.

She'd only been trying to help, but, thinking back, of course she'd hurt his pride. He'd made a point of avoiding her after that, and heaven knew back then she hadn't been used to being ignored. Consequently, whenever she'd had the opportunity, she'd pestered him to get a reaction. *Any* reaction. Give the guy his due, he had never once lashed out.

"You still haven't told me your name."

The rich timbre of his voice swept her back to the present. He'd moved into the kitchen.

"I'm Nina," she said, and as he flicked a faucet to wash his hands she caught the smirk. Her senses sharpened. "Something wrong with my name?"

"Just the last Nina I knew was as thin as two sticks and went around with a perpetual scowl on her face."

An ex? It didn't sound as if they'd blasted too far off the launching pad. Still, a man with his attributes wouldn't have pined for long.

Sauntering back, Gabriel swept the first aid kit off the ledge. Moving past, he took a seat at the foot of the bed and began to sort through bandages and lotions.

"So, Nina, how do you know the groom? You're not an old flame here to cause trouble?" He looked up, almost hopeful. "Are you?"

"We've never met."

The square angle of his jaw shifted. "You're not a friend of the bride or the groom, yet you're attending their wedding?"

She cleared her throat, formed words in her mind to explain her situation, but those words would not leave her mouth. She *wanted* to tell him. She needed to. She certainly couldn't lie about who she was.

He dabbed a cotton ball with antiseptic, and indicated with a tip of his chin that she should sit too.

"I've got it," he said. "You're a wedding planner. One of the experts people hire to make sure everything's perfect on the day."

Smothering a sigh, she shook her head and joined him.

The line between his brows furrowed again. "You really don't want me to dig any more, do you?"

"It's not that exactly…"

"Look, if you're more comfortable sticking with Nina the Mysterious for now, I'll back off. Privacy can be a huge issue, I know."

She opened her mouth to fess up, but something held her back.

The thing was…she wasn't *sure* who she was any more. With each passing day she wondered more. Being here with this delectable man only seemed to confuse the matter. She was a waitress, yet he was treating her like a princess. Once she *had* been a princess, of sorts, but then her family had lost everything and, not long after, she'd lost her position. Much of her identity had been lost with it.

The truth was she *would* rather remain Nina the Mysterious for now. Lately she'd felt so exposed and raw and vulnerable… She wasn't certain she could stand to peel off one more layer—even to the man who'd saved her life.

Not that she was embarrassed that she'd taken a waitressing job. She would rather step up any day than lie around fanning herself and hoping for some miracle to materialise and get her out of this jam. If she was embarrassed about anything it was that her performance here could have been better. If she was going to stay—and for now she had to—the other staff were right: she needed to take it up a gear.

As if agreeing to put an end to the identity discussion, he nodded at her foot. "Let's fix you up."

He first applied antiseptic to the bump on her head, then to her ankle. A large adhesive bandage was fitted, and a crepe one wound around that. When he was done, she ran two fingers over the joint—which didn't feel nearly as sore as it had.

"Don't have much in the way of other provisions." He pushed on his thighs to stand. "Some bread and spread, if you're hungry. And I do have a bottle of quite passable red wine."

Watching firelight flicker behind his silhouette, shifting ever darkening shapes over the roughly hewn walls, she felt she didn't need another thing other than that fire's heat, this blessed mattress, and her host's not unpleasant company. Despite the sexual awareness bubbling away below the surface—or perhaps because of it—she hadn't felt this stress-free in ages. Being stranded with a gorgeous man clearly worked for her. Why not go for broke?

She smiled on a nod. "A glass of wine would be nice."

In the kitchen, he opened the bottle of red and dug out a packet of peanuts and filled a ceramic bowl.

"Here's a not so interesting fact," he said sauntering back. "When I was a kid I wanted to run a macadamia nut farm."

"Well, I think that's *very* interesting." She accepted a glass and he poured. "I wanted to own a ballet school. What happened to your dream?"

He hesitated in pouring. "I'm not sure. Maybe I should put it on my 'to-do' list."

He raised his glass, she raised hers, and they sipped. The wine was mellow, and trailed warmth from her throat to her belly. Repositioning her weight, she leaned back on one elbow and sipped again.

"So," he said, getting comfortable beside her, "you dance?"

She screwed up her nose. "I was awful. I just liked the costumes."

Grinning, he grabbed some peanuts from the bowl which he'd set between them. "What else do you like?"

"You'll laugh."

"All the better."

"I like boxing."

He spluttered, and hit his chest to help clear his throat. "Didn't you see *Million Dollar Baby?*"

"Not competition boxing. Just mucking around." She protected her chin and jabbed the air. "At the gym." She shrugged. "I'm improving."

Her ankle throbbed once, and pain spiked up her shin. Careful of her wine, she manoeuvred back until she lay on her side, her cheek resting in one palm.

Better.

"What about you?" she asked. "Ever put on the gloves?"

"Nope. But I've tried practically every other sport."

"A figures man crossed with an athlete? I'm seeing that turbo-blasting calculator guy again."

"Ballet and boxing. We all have another side."

She took a long sip. *We sure do.*

"How's the ankle?" he asked, shaking some peanuts in his palm and throwing them back into his mouth.

"Much better."

Chewing, he evaluated the weather through the window. "The rain's set in."

She finished his thought. "And we should bunk down here for the night?"

"Don't know that there's an alternative. The resort doctor can check your head and leg tomorrow." His grin was crooked, and criminally sexy. "I think you'll make it past dawn."

"Thanks to you."

When she smiled over her glass at him, a double-knot in Gabriel's chest yanked tight.

More than ever before he was head-down, needing to ensure that the professional gamble he'd taken turned into a goldmine. Nothing at any point in his career had mattered more, and he'd learned that success meant keeping your eye on the ball. Always.

But as he watched his mysterious Nina in the fireglow—shadow and light playing over her heart-shaped face—a distracting something tugged inside of him. Something intense and pleasant and real.

She was beautiful, certainly—although he doubted she was aware of the power of her smile or how expressive and bright her eyes were. Her body was strong, yet wholly feminine. Sensual. She was all woman.

As she looked up from her glass and back towards the crackling fire—her drying hair splayed over her shoulder—more than physical attraction spoke to him. Even as he instinctively hardened in anticipation of enjoying another kiss or three, an added influence whispered in his ear.

He wanted to put a name to it, but the only word that came to mind hardly fitted. Trust was earned over a lifetime. Something he didn't ask for and rarely gave away.

Still, whatever it was that stirred him up about Nina, it felt good. Even if straight-out lust was way less complicated.

He prised his gaze from her lips and found his feet. "More wine?"

She made a purring sound in her throat, and her heavy-lidded gaze met his. She stretched her good leg straight along the mattress and replied, "Half a glass. Any more after that bath and I might go to sleep."

Relieving her of her glass, he skirted the bed and found the bottle. He poured her half, filled his up, then found a handtowel to mop up the few drops spilled on the cedar table.

"There's a creek out the back of here, filled with fish and some platypus. Or is that platypi?" He rounded the bed and, keeping an eye on his over-full glass, sat carefully down. "I was thinking this afternoon when I first saw you that this place reminds me of a spot my aunt took me on vacation once when I was a kid…"

His words trailed off.

Her arm was stretched out over the quilt, one cheek lying on that inside elbow. Her lips were slightly parted. If he spoke loudly enough she would rouse, but her breathing said she was already on her way to dreamtime. An experience like the one she'd endured today would knock it out of anyone. Couple that with a relaxing soak and glass of good wine…

Still, he was disappointed sleep had taken her so quickly.

His gaze slid down her tranquil form and he gnawed

his lower lip. What should he do about those legs? The wolf inside wanted to leave them exposed, but the reluctant gentleman said she might catch a chill.

Setting down the glasses, he eased the quilt over her body, covering her legs and those peach-tipped toes. Then, so as not to disturb her, he placed the chair before the fire, which had grown to a vigorous state. Stretching the cranky muscles in his legs, he threaded fingers behind his head and clicked his thoughts over to its usual fare. To work. To that crucial venture.

To this island.

After investing so much in this project, his efforts to set this place back well on its feet couldn't fail. Anything that didn't work towards the reestablishment of a healthy profit margin would be culled. Nothing that worked against success would be tolerated. His involvement here must have one outcome and one outcome only.

Absolute success.

He filed figures through his mind—advertising budgets, staff payrolls. Where to cut, where to spend…

But his gaze kept wandering to his slumbering kitten, to the gentle rise and fall of her chest beneath that chequered shirt. He had to let her sleep, and yet with every passing moment—with every whisper at his ear—that new tug inside of him kept willing her awake.

CHAPTER FIVE

NINA dreamed of a tidal wave, a colossal giant that made this afternoon's rollers look like dwarfs.

The wave in her dream curled up, throwing its enormous shadow over her, before crashing an inch behind her running heels. Having thought she was clear of danger, she cried out when its cold fingers coiled around her ankles and dragged her back. She screamed, but she knew no matter what she did, however hard she tried, this time she was a goner.

As the wave overcame her she was drawn down into the churning, bubbling wash. The motion jerked and pushed her. She couldn't breathe, couldn't find the surface. Then something gripped her shoulder, trying to lift her out. Needing precious air, she groped above her head, reaching for the wavering reflections dancing on the water's surface and the shadow waiting beyond that.

Nina's eyes popped open at the same time as she sucked down a desperate gulp of oxygen.

She felt pressure on her shoulder, took in her shadowy surrounds, then heard her name murmured in a gravelled voice. The floating pieces of the jigsaw clicked together and, heart thumping, she rolled over.

In the dying firelight, Gabriel sat on the edge of the bed, one knee angled over the sheet, concern lining his handsome face. As his gaze roamed her brow, her cheek, she remembered her scream from the dream and knew she must have cried out.

Emptying her bursting lungs, she touched her forehead and patted the damp away. "I dreamt I was drowning and you saved me."

A sultry grin sparkled in his eyes. "That wasn't a dream. Here—push up." He helped her to straighten higher on the bed, eased the sheet up, then pulled the quilt around her neck. "You're safe now. Go back to sleep."

In her mind Nina relieved the moment he'd dragged her out of the wash and laid her upon that sandy knoll. Thank God he'd been there.

She hugged the quilt tight.

Thank God he was here now. For the first time in weeks she *did* feel safe and certain.

Lighter rain pattered on the roof. She rubbed one eye, then glanced out of the window. Still dark, but no morning bird calls echoed through the bush outside. How long had she slept?

Gabriel had moved to the fireplace to stir the embers. The room smelled of firewood warmth—the kind electric blankets and heaters couldn't compete with.

Over one broad shoulder, his gaze hooked hers. "You're wide awake now, aren't you?"

She nodded and shifted higher.

"Are you hungry?" he asked, replacing the poker. "Thirsty?"

She wasn't hungry in the least, but… "I'd love a glass of water."

He brought a large glass over, and she drank it down without stopping.

"Better?" he asked when she handed the empty glass back.

"Much. Thank you."

She wiggled and got more comfortable. She felt positively toasty. A little sore from her struggles earlier, but also beautifully rested. This unpretentious atmosphere certainly helped.

"Why did you rent this place?" she asked as he slid the glass onto the side table.

She'd already surmised that he must like to rough it, and she was aware of this cabin's charm, but what deeper reason did he have for preferring bare essentials to the luxury available down the way? Had he played Davy Crockett as a boy? Perhaps he longed to be a social hermit, like Howard Hughes? But then why come to this island at all? Australia's isolated Outback might be a better choice.

He shrugged, and in a trick of the fading firelight his chest seemed to grow before her eyes.

"I had the wedding to come to here, and some business to attend to, but in between I wanted to take the opportunity to really get away. I haven't done that since I was a kid." He nodded at the bed. "Mind if I sit down?" He rubbed his butt. "That chair's not meant for catching zeds."

Without a second thought she moved over, and the mattress dipped as he joined her. He stretched one denim-clad leg down over the quilt; the other foot he rested on the floorboards.

"What kind of kid were you?" she asked, snuggling back down into the pillows, hands clasped under her cheek.

"Typical, I guess. Sometimes lonely. What about you?"

Definitely not lonely. She'd had plenty of friends.

Plenty to keep her occupied. Singing and dancing lessons. An interest in art. "You could've probably summed me up as confident." She wouldn't say *cocky*.

His chuckle warmed her more. "I have no trouble imagining that."

She recalled her idyllic past, how she hadn't wanted for a thing, but couldn't settle on the feeling those memories gave her. "It seems so long ago now…like that girl was someone else." Her mouth tugged to one side and she sighed. That Nina *had* been someone else.

"Sounds as if you'd like to go back."

"Yes. And no." She pushed up onto an elbow. "What I'd like to know is who I'm meant to be now. Who I'll be in the future." She relaxed the tension biting between her shoulders, and almost succeeded in keeping the embarrassment from her voice. "Too much information."

"I'm all for honesty."

Nina blinked over, and watched him watching the firelight. He liked the truth? Maybe she should give it to him. There was something about the intimacy of being surrounded by lush, tropical vegetation, that gave her the courage to try.

"Those questions never bothered me until recently," she ventured. "I had a set of goalposts in my mind—" to be a huge success in publishing "—and I was headed straight for the middle."

"Then something knocked the wind out of you?"

"Exactly."

She'd lost her job, but she might as well have been ploughed down and kicked in the gut. She'd never felt insecure before that, even when her mother had blown the Petrelle money. She'd been angry, yes, and disappointed at such waste. But ultimately she'd known she had her own abilities to rely upon.

Then her livelihood had been ripped out from under her and her confidence had been shaken to her core. She'd felt physically winded for days. But she'd forced herself out from beneath the covers, had mailed résumés off and returned to the gym. She'd promised herself things would work out. She *would* get back on her feet and eventually kick a winning goal right through the centre of those posts.

Only those posts seemed so far away now.

"Worse things have happened in my life," she continued, peering into the flames and remembering her brother's and father's deaths. "But I'd always held it together—"

Stinging emotion filled her throat and she had to stop and swallow. She felt his gaze on her.

"Want to tell me about it?"

Her cheeks hot, she shook her head. She'd said enough. If she said any more she might cry, and that wasn't something she liked to do too often.

"It's nothing that a million other people haven't faced."

"Maybe you're trying too hard not to disappoint other people?" he said. "Or trying too hard not to disappoint yourself. Cut yourself a break. Give it time. I see a strength in you I don't see in too many people."

She coughed out a laugh. "You saw that strength *when?* While I was trapped and screaming for help?"

He slid down a little. With his forehead near hers, their noses all but touching, he mock-frowned at her. "Did you hear the part about cutting yourself a break?"

Her gaze lowered to his mouth, and her own lips tingled with want. His scent was so intoxicating…the temptation to taste him again so strong…

But he moved away and, resting against the bedhead,

threaded his fingers behind his head. Man, he had *the* best set of biceps.

"You said yourself," he told her, "most people face a crisis. More than one. But no one knows what their most vulnerable spot is until fate uncovers it. Recovering from a meltdown can take time, but then you shape up even stronger. Whatever it is you're facing—" he winked across at her "—you'll be okay."

It sounded as if he knew what he was talking about, and, despite feeling low a lot of the time here, this experience *had* toughened her up. She'd found new ways to adapt. New qualities to admire—in others as well as herself.

Still, she couldn't help wincing as a prickly knot formed low in her stomach.

You'll be okay.

She sighed. "I wish I could believe that."

She must have sounded pathetically in need of TLC, because next she knew his arm was around her shoulder and he'd urged her cheek to rest against the slope of his hot bare chest. His fingers trailed up and down her arm before he gave her an encouraging squeeze. "I'll believe in you."

She blew out a quiet breath and, happy to surrender, curled in. With him holding her, his warm breath stirring her hair, anything seemed possible.

Now she'd shared so much, would he open up too?

She hesitated then asked, "Can I ask what your crisis was?"

He exhaled slowly. "I lost someone close. Someone who had faith in me when he didn't need to."

With his voice rumbling against her ear, her heart squeezed for him. Was there anything more difficult than saying goodbye for ever to someone you loved?

"For a long time I felt stuck, wanting to go back and change things," he said, and his hand unconsciously tightened on her arm. "I let that person down."

"I can't imagine you ever letting anyone down." Her palm skimmed higher, to rest where his heartbeat boomed. "You should try to remember why that person had faith in you."

"I never quite worked that one out. But I'll never forget it."

His tone was low and painfully earnest. As far as confessions went, that was a doozy. He seemed so capable; someone to rely on. So where had such an admission come from? Had he confessed that to anyone before? Instinct said not.

She pressed her ear to his heartbeat and, closing her eyes, willed her belief in him to soak through.

Then she smiled. "I might have a solution."

"Tell me." His words were patient, amused.

"Let someone have faith in you again." The same way he said he'd believe in her.

But when he stiffened, a shrivelling feeling fell through her middle. He'd opened up, but clearly she'd overstepped the mark. She hadn't meant to imply he was in any way unreliable, if that was how he'd taken it. So many people must count on him every day in his business life, for starters.

But then he breathed again, deeper than before, and when his arm moved higher his fingers brushed hair away from her face.

"What does having faith mean to you?" he asked, as the embers flickered lower and the room darkened more, cocooning them in their own little world.

"Loyalty," she replied, relieved he didn't sound defensive. "Commitment. Trust."

"Trust…"

When his mouth brushed her crown her pulse quickened, and her nipples hardened beneath the stiff fabric of her shirt. His arm urged her closer, and the growth of his day-old beard rasped over her. As her heart galloped high in her chest his mouth touched her hair, and anticipation sucked through her veins like a thousand-degree backdraft.

"I'd like for *you* to trust me," he said, and he turned her slightly in his arms. But she felt so overwhelmed, her pulse was racing so fast, she couldn't meet his eyes.

They'd kissed on the beach, but that had been different; she'd been swept up in the high-risk animation of the moment. But now every cell in her body was acutely aware of what lay beyond this caress. With each word and enticing touch he'd let her know his intentions. He wanted her to trust him. Enough to take this next step.

A thumb strummed an inch below one shoulderblade. When his chin made its way with an agonising lack of speed across her brow down her cheek to her jaw—when the delicious contrast of his lips whispered over hers—Nina felt so light-headed and doused with desire she wondered if she might faint. Then his mouth parted, feathering over hers, and her core caught light.

More than anything she'd ever wanted, she wanted him to kiss her now. Intensely.

Completely.

"I want to make love to you," he said, and that thumb travelled down the dent of her back. He kneaded the dip at the base of her spine as his teeth nipped and tugged her lower lip. "I want to make love to you like I've never wanted to make love to anyone before."

The gravelled timbre of those words pulled a final

trigger. Mouthwatering hunger flooded her centre, and her body reflexively bowed towards his. But the nerves in her throat were convulsing so badly she couldn't trust herself to speak. So she combed her fingers over the sandpaper of his jaw and let her eyes and her trembling want speak for her.

He turned his head slightly to kiss her palm, then, cupping her bottom, scooped her in while his lips slowly circled over hers. When the thick ridge of his erection ground against her belly, creamy warmth dampened her inside thighs.

"I want all of you," he told her, and then his mouth claimed hers and the velvet heat of his tongue pushed deep inside.

He kissed her for heady, blistering moments, breaking off briefly to murmur again, "I want to feel all of you, taste all of you." His fingers curved around the back of her thigh, between her legs. "Every inch and all night."

Turned inside out, she shook with maddening need. If he wanted her—wanted her all night—she wanted him more.

As they slipped further down the bed he systematically released each button of her shirt. When the last was undone, and she was quivering from head to foot, the backs of his fingers brushed up the curls at the apex of her thighs before drifting higher to trace over her belly.

His eyes found hers, and as his gaze glowed across he wound fabric around two fingers and slid one half of her shirt fully open. His head cocked as he examined the swell of her breast in the firelight, then he rolled her on her back and drove down both sides of the shirt, until the sleeves hung halfway down her arms. His gaze burned over her breasts, then ran a deliberate line of fire all the way down. When, as if more than satisfied, he raised his chin, her lips parted to take in more air.

Where would he kiss her next? The sensitive sides of her waist? The smouldering tips of her breasts? Or would his mouth caress the intimate folds that ached for so much of his touch? Every inch of her begged for the caress of his mouth, the skilled flick and curl of his tongue.

His palm traced up her side and found her breast. The pad of his thumb circled the areola before he gently pinched the tip. She writhed against the sheets and her hand automatically reached to hold his. His hand folded hers back at the same time as his mouth came down, tasting and then laving her nipple, as if it were dipped in thick honey.

Her breathing ragged, she held his head and slipped her good leg around the back of his thigh. His teeth clamped her nipple, and as he drew slowly back she arced with him until he released her to move off the bed.

He unzipped, denim fell, and her eyes rounded. She was more than ready for him; her body was a hop-scotch of lit firecrackers waiting to explode. But the sight of his heavy rigid shaft dried her mouth. Everything about Gabriel was larger than life.

Joining her, he eased her up slightly in order to peel the fabric completely from her arms. He tossed the shirt, then lay beside her. In the dancing shadows he searched her eyes. A lazy finger trailed down the side of her ribs, over her hip, and drew a leisurely circle around her navel before his hot palm flattened against her belly. She bit her lip and shut her eyes as his touch delved and slipped between her thighs. When his fingers rode back up and stroked her with just the right pressure, to create just the right burn, she focused inward, concentrating on the rising tide.

With her mind filled with bright darting lights, his mouth covered hers—not gently this time; his tongue probed so thoroughly she wondered if he needed more from her than she could give. But to know the unbridled depth of his desire felt intoxicating. Felt wickedly, wonderfully right.

Her fingers combed up the back of his head, flexing through his hair before sculpting down the sides of his face so she could lock his kiss to hers. She wanted to sear these emotions in her mind…the feel of his jaw working with hers…his magnificent chest grazing her breasts.

She was perched on the teetering brink of release when the kiss ended, a second too soon. He took her wrist, kissing the inside before he moved to position himself above her. Holding her eyes with his, he eased in the tip of his erection, and reflexively her muscles clenched to draw more of him inside.

He began to move, filling her, caressing her. Surrendering to sensation, she fanned her palms over his shoulders as her head rocked back, driving into the pillow. The intensity left perspiration on her brow…left her brilliantly, blissfully out of her mind.

Her nails dug in as she craned up to kiss his chest, so steamy and strong, and all hers for the night.

I knew it would be like this, she thought. This was more than two bodies joining…this was so much more than just sex.

He nipped her chin, thrust again, and hit a spot so high and deep the jolt and thrill tore a sob from her chest. The tremors building in the base of her belly quickened as her throat ached and moisture filled the corners of her eyes. The intensity of pleasure was too much to contain.

She held the hair either side of his temples and, teetering on the edge, thought again, *Are you real?*

He answered her by taking her lips, and when the stroke of his kiss melded seamlessly with the rhythm of his hips the ticking time bomb at her centre compressed and shone, supernova bright.

She began to fold in on herself. With all the world fading away his body braced above hers and the muscles in his big shoulders bunched. When his head craned back, and he bared his teeth at the sky, she felt him shudder and empty his energy inside of her.

Her own tremors rose higher…soaring, spiking.

Peaking.

The instant a thousand waves crashed in at once he groaned, and drank his name from her lips.

CHAPTER SIX

ONCE was only the beginning.

They made love again, and a third time, and as the rain eased and the yellow fingers of dawn reached through that single window pane Nina snuggled back into the incomparable warmth of her lover.

Gabriel sat at the head of the bed, his back against the rest, his powerful arms coiled around her waist. She sat between his legs, her head slanted against his chest, her arms wrapped around his. The previous hours had raced by as if they'd only been minutes.

Tomorrow was almost here.

His chin brushed over her crown and she felt him harden against the small of her back. Teasing, she wriggled against him. "Aren't you sick of me yet?"

"Nope." His expert mouth found the sweep of her neck. Goosebumps erupted down her right side as his teeth danced over the still wanting sweep of skin. He whispered at her ear, "Stay with me."

She froze, then blinked several times. Had she heard right?

"What do you mean, stay?"

He hummed at her temple. "Here. With me."

What a crazy, wonderful idea, but… "Gabriel, I can't."

"Sure you can." He urged her face around and kissed her thoroughly. Her lips felt swollen from his all-night attention, but she only melted again now. Kissing, in all its forms, was his absolute forte.

The kiss broke softly. With a growl in his throat, he circled the tip of her nose with his.

"Stay."

She fisted her hand against his chest. Oh, God, how she wanted to. "It's not that easy."

The light in his gaze dimmed, and for the first time she saw something else in his eyes…something hard and close to unforgiving.

His voice dropped enough to make her shiver. "Is there someone else?"

"Of course not," she shot back, and the light in his eyes faded back up.

"In that case…" he edged her around more "…let me convince you."

Holding her chin in the vee of one hand, he tipped her back until she lay flat. The line of kisses he dropped down to her cleavage blew fresh life into embers wanting to flash hot again. And when his mouth tasted one tender nipple, and his tongue wove down to her midriff, her hands stretched towards him and her fingers twined through his hair.

She wanted to stay—so much that it hurt. But the idea was ridiculous. For one, as long as her ankle held up, she had a shift later today. Which led to a far bigger problem. Gabriel had no idea who she was. Or who she *wasn't*. He'd given her the option of remaining Nina the Mysterious, and at the time withholding her identity had seemed the easier, more attractive option. But that had been before they'd slept together.

The last few hours had seemed surreal. She could

almost convince herself she was just another rich guest enjoying a no-consequences holiday fling with a gorgeous playboy. But of course that dream couldn't last. She couldn't stay. Inevitably they would see each other at the resort and her secret would be out.

She pinched the bridge of her nose to stem the sting of emotion.

Okay. She would simply tell him now. Come clean with everything. Then the ball would be back in his court. He'd said, *I'll believe in you.* Not light words. If it hadn't been a line, he deserved the chance to prove he'd meant it. Prove to her that her faith in him wasn't built purely on firelight and fantasy.

Willing her heart to quit crashing against her ribs, she found a rational voice. "Gabriel, there's something I need to tell you."

His tongue twirled languidly around her navel.

She gripped his arms and tried to pull him up. "Are you listening?"

His mouth only dropped lower. "I can multi-task."

She didn't doubt it. "There's more you need to know."

He grazed all the way up, until his eyes twinkled directly into hers. "All I need to know is…" he tasted her chin "…I want to be with you."

He said it so easily. As if this could really mean more than a night or two if she let it. But she had to face facts. Clearly Gabriel was no novice at this kind of encounter. He'd known what he wanted and he'd set out to get it. She'd be crazy to believe this interlude meant anything more to him than a dab of icing on his holiday cake; she'd seen enough of his I'm-kicking-back-on-vacation type to know. Hell, rather than irritated, he might be *pleased* to discover she was a waitress. The thanks-and-sorry-it-didn't-work-out would be easier that way.

She realised he was looking deeply into her eyes.

A fingertip stroked her cheek. "Hey, what's wrong?"

She sighed. *Oh, just everything.*

"Gabriel…" She tried to find the right words to begin. "This day has been unbelievable. You make me feel so good. *Too* good."

A sexy smile tugged the corner of his mouth before he suckled a line up her throat to her lips. "Trust me. There's no such thing as too good."

Nina woke with a start.

Blinking open her eyes, she remembered the rain… the hideaway cabin in the bush. Foremost she remembered waking in the midnight hours, and how Gabriel's soft, skilled mouth and hard, practised body had claimed hers again and again.

Her every fibre lit up and tingled, recalling the bone-melting orgasms he'd given her. The way his tongue and hands had endlessly explored. She'd mindlessly given herself over to every wondrous stroke and squeeze.

Then he'd asked her to stay.

Her stomach somersaulted. She turned over, tried to focus her sleep-deprived brain, and realised she was alone amid the tangle of sheets. Where was Gabriel? She'd got severely sidetracked last night, but they still had a conversation to finish.

She had a confession to make.

Unfortunately talking quietly in romantic firelight was a far cry from coming clean in the cold light of day. She wasn't a wealthy guest at Diamond Shores. She worked at the resort. She'd let Gabriel believe what he'd wanted about her identity, but now she needed to speak up.

He was attracted to her. He wanted this holiday fling to continue. Only he had no idea who the woman he was making love with was. Hell, *she* didn't know who she was any more—or who'd she'd be next week. Next year.

Nina eased out of bed. Bringing a sheet along, she limped to the window. She had to believe he wouldn't be upset by her news. They'd spent a glorious night together. Precious time not every couple got to enjoy.

She stopped by the window. He didn't appear to be outside. When he hadn't returned after a few minutes she removed her bandage and drew a bath. As she slipped into the warm water she fantasised about him sneaking in and surprising her. But when the bath cooled, she dried and dressed again in the shirt Gabriel had stripped from her late last night. She finger-brushed her teeth with some paste she found while her stomach knotted.

She needed to get this off her chest. How much longer would he be?

Through the smudge of glass, and a break in the canopy of palms and vines, a flawless dome of blue smiled down. The leaves looked greener, hanging low and heavy with morning dew. While the air had felt chilly last night, heat was already building inside the cabin. Another tropical day in paradise.

She'd felt so down of late. In limbo. Lost. Feeling alive again last night had felt so real! The light and smell and sound of everything had seemed amplified. Brighter. She wanted to feel that alive again, and now she knew how to make that happen.

Not by continuing this charade with Gabriel; hiding behind a fantasy, no matter how wonderful, wasn't the answer. She had to step up and get her life back on track as quickly as possible. Until that opportunity arose, she'd put one hundred and ten percent into doing the best job she could here. Put her all into winning even a little respect from her co-workers.

Hope. A real belief that she could regain her pride. Her beautiful night here with Gabriel had given her that.

Her stomach growled. She'd eaten nothing but a handful of nuts since a scant salad yesterday at lunch. When a fruit bowl caught her eye, she chose an apple and chomped as she made her way aimlessly around.

She was about to make herself a coffee when a movement outside caught her eye. She tipped closer to the window and peered out.

Three…no, four wallabies!

When she swung open the door, air, fresh and minty, filled her lungs. She breathed deeply, listening to a symphony of birds, their squawks and chirps and whistles echoing off the treetops and jutting cliffs. To her left, the wallabies' ears turned in her direction.

Three were sunning themselves, resting on their sides on a nearby red and black-patched ledge. The fourth had a joey in her pouch; Nina held her breath as two tiny ears and a black nose twitched from the soft furry purse on its mother's tummy. They were similar to, but far smaller than, their marsupial kangaroo cousins. Their petite jaws munched rhythmically, and Nina longed to furrow her fingers through the thick brown fur of the curved backs. Their strong tails, which ended with a white tip, seemed to go on for ever.

Careful not to startle them, she bit off some apple, crept closer, then lobbed the fruit over. The mother used her tail and small front paws to edge away in the opposite direction. The others twitched their ears, but didn't deign to turn their onyx long-lashed gazes towards their visitor. She sat on a nearby boulder, and after a time one wallaby rocked slowly over. It collected the apple in its paws and ignored her while it chewed.

This same scene would have existed fifty years ago. A *hundred* and fifty years ago. How peaceful it would be to live here without television or the internet, Nina thought. No sales pitches or rush-rush schedules. Just the gentle sights and sounds of timeless nature.

She was about to throw more apple when the wallabies straightened, fully alert. Their ears pricked up and then they bounded off, their tails acting as precision springboards. As they disappeared over the rocks and into the bush Nina heard it too—a motor, distant, but coming this way.

She perched upon the wallabies' ledge and waited to greet her arrival. A few moments later Gabriel appeared, wheeling in a motorbike. Nothing large and mean— rather a fun ride, with chunky tyres obviously meant for off-road.

He stopped when he saw her, and his eyes opened in surprise. "You're up."

She eased off the ledge. "You were up earlier."

He performed a flourishing bow. "Your limousine, *madame.*"

She laughed, but with a touch of irony. She hadn't ridden in a limousine for a very long time.

He kicked down the bike's stand, whipped a carry-bag off the handlebars and closed the distance separating them in three long strides. Then arms that felt like heaven gathered her in and his mouth dropped over hers. As one hand edged up to cradle and faintly rotate the back of her head, Nina dissolved into their best kiss yet. Her fingers fanned up to knead the muscle beneath his fresh jersey knit shirt.

His lips left hers reluctantly, coming back to sip again before he deftly took her hand and began to lead her inside. Her mind stopped spinning enough for her to pull up. She wouldn't be distracted again. Before he swept her up into the clouds again they needed to talk. He needed to know this was no run-of-the-mill holiday fling. She needed to lay her cards on the table and own up to who she was…or at least who she wasn't.

When she stopped, he stopped too, a frown tugging at his brows. Then he shook his head as if to clear it.

"I'm an idiot." He swooped her up into his arms. "I forgot your ankle. I'll carry you."

Nina fought the impulse to hold onto him. His no-argument brand of chivalry was intoxicating, but… "My ankle's *fine*."

He wasn't listening. Instead he moved with her towards the open cabin door.

He stepped over the threshold, and a sense of *déjà vu* filtered through her. Had so much time passed since that sudden rainstorm yesterday? They were here again, standing in the exact same spot, and he was just as imposing and commanding and delicious as ever.

But he wasn't heading for the bed. He was looking down at her with a mix of desire and depth and…

Trust?

She cleared the lump from her throat and took a breath. Now or never.

"Last night," she began, "you asked if I wanted to stay."

He nodded.

She blew out a breath. "Well, Gabriel—see, it's like this—"

"You want to go back to the resort, don't you?" His jaw tightened. "You're missing the spa tubs and silver service."

"God, *no*. That's not it at all."

His brows snapped together. "You don't like the resort?"

"If you really want to know…" She scrunched her nose and shook her head. *Not a bit.*

A pulse in his cheek started to tick and his jaw shifted to one side. "So what's wrong with it?"

Nina was taken aback. That stony look and tone… Suddenly he seemed so serious. About her dislike of the resort?

He'd said he'd taken this cabin to get away from it all. She'd believed him. But his questions and the intense glint in his eye didn't sit with his carefree "escape into the wilderness" story. Something didn't add up.

He wanted to know what was wrong with the resort?

She quizzed him. "Maybe you should tell *me?*"

He blinked several times before his chin tucked in. "Why would I do that?"

"Because I'm getting the feeling you don't like Diamond Shores so much either."

His pupils dilated, swallowing the pale irises until his eyes appeared almost black. "I'm simply interested."

He crossed the room, sat her on the chair, but she stood straight back up.

His ears were pink with irritation, and there was a weird, distant look in his eye. She wasn't mistaken. There was far more to his questions than simple interest. Did he trust her enough to tell her what was wrong?

Maybe if she gave him a chance to thaw out?

She collected the bottle off the counter to make two strong coffees. But when she screwed the lid it wouldn't budge. She clamped the bottle under one arm and twisted hard. Stuck fast.

In the meantime, Gabriel had frowned over. "Are you staying on the island with friends?"

She sighed. *If only.*

She took a hesitant step nearer. He sounded so gruff. "Why do you want to know?"

"Because I need to know what people are saying. What they're *thinking.*"

When he thumped his fist against the wall she jumped. Then he growled under his breath, something about, "…hiding out here…playing Huck Finn… should be back there, making changes…"

With worry choking off her breath, she slowly brought the bottle close to her chest. "Gabriel…what are you talking about?"

Letting out a defeated breath, he sank into the chair.

"I bought this island a week ago," he ground out. "It's on the brink of bankruptcy, and I'm here to make sure everything and everyone who doesn't perform is eliminated." He lifted his chin. "Pronto."

The coffee bottle slipped from her hands, smashed, and shattered to pieces. As the crash ricocheted off the walls, Gabriel shot to his feet. The way Nina's face had paled, the way her hands clutched at her throat, she might have thrown a javelin that had missed his heart by an inch.

She stared blindly at the mess at her feet, then fixed her huge topaz-coloured eyes on his.

"I broke the bottle," she croaked out, and when her lashes blinked he thought he saw her eyes glisten.

This wasn't the reaction he'd expected. He hadn't wanted three cheers, but owning Diamond Shores wasn't chickenfeed. Or it wasn't to him. His announcement was at least worth a sentence or two of recognition. Still, God knew how much Nina's family was worth. Owning an island might well seem inconsequential to many of the guests who stayed here.

He ground his back teeth and ploughed a hand through his hair. It frustrated the hell out of him. Regardless of how far he'd come, there were still times when he felt like someone's poor relation.

Nina was concentrating on the mess on the floor, as if she couldn't get her mind around how to clean it up.

Rubbing the back of his neck, he moved forward. "Don't worry about that." There was more to worry about than an old broken bottle.

But she didn't seem to hear. Instead her hands covered her face. "Oh, God, what a mess."

He took her hands from her cheeks.

"It's okay," he said more gently. "I'll get someone in to clean it up." But she wound out of his hold, stooped and began to pick up the pieces. He hunkered down and eased the glass from her hand. "You don't need to do that." When she collected another piece, he held her wrist. "*Nina,* I'll get a maid in from the resort."

Biting her lip, she stood and spun away, her hands bracing the counter. "We should go. We should go *now.*"

He tugged an earlobe and groaned.

Okay. He had an idea what was wrong.

Stepping closer, he cupped her shoulders. "Don't be embarrassed. Yes, I own the island, but I'm glad you told me how unhappy you are with the resort."

When he'd arrived three days ago he'd introduced

himself to key people but had insisted that his true identity be kept from the rest of the staff. He wanted to experience April's wedding and the resort incognito. He'd also made it clear he needed to be informed of every suggestion for improvements and all complaints.

After he'd jogged to the resort this morning, to bring back some wheels, he'd dropped in to his bungalow and had been greeted by an avalanche of messages. Various managers wanted his ear. One guest had complained he'd been injured—the result of an incompetent ski-boat driver. A celebrity wedding had been cancelled; the bride had heard rumours regarding "off" seafood. The music at the nightclub wasn't exciting enough. The childminders weren't any fun.

And so it went on.

A meeting was scheduled for the day before he flew back to Sydney—Monday. He and the managers would crunch figures and implement a kick-butt game plan. But this morning he hadn't wanted to face the hassle. Face the possibility that this time he might have gone beyond his limits. He'd only wanted to get back to Nina and re-ignite the fires which had raged within these walls last night.

She affected him like a drug, and he wanted to enjoy that all-over high again and again. But he'd been an idiot, a coward, to buy into that distraction. His captivating lover also happened to be a guest at Diamond Shores—a guest who'd admitted in the plainest of terms how dissatisfied she was with the facilities. Talk about a wake-up call.

Every day, every *minute* counted towards getting this resort back on its feet.

He moved to collect the parcel bag he'd brought in.

Nina was right. They needed to go.

"I put your clothes in to be laundered. I had one of the boutique managers—"

"Whose name did you use?"

To clean her clothes?

He frowned. "Mine."

Surely she wasn't concerned about a pair of cut-offs? Although second-hand-looking fashion could be sexy.

He retrieved a wrap and a one-piece from the bag.

So, too, was designer fashion.

From the bottom of the bag he handed over a pair of sunglasses. Her eyes rounded and a puff of wind left her lungs; he might have handed her a priceless jewel.

"I've seen these in the window. They're Bulgari." She pointed out the arms. "Those are real diamonds."

As if on autopilot, she slipped them on and moved to the window to check her reflection. He was feeling somewhat redeemed, thinking about how big a bonus to give that astute boutique manager, when Nina's shoulders came down and she lowered the shades.

She turned back with a sombre face. "I can't accept these."

He gave her a sidelong look. "You don't like them?"

"I *love* them."

"Then don't be modest."

Although he did admire that quality. Women he dated were often eager to hear about gifts—the more expensive the better. When they started talking diamond rings, he stopped calling. He'd had no time for that kind of commitment. He had less time now.

"It's not modesty." She joined him and handed the glasses back. "Not really."

His laugh was edgy. "Nina, you're confusing me."

She inhaled deeply, then her gaze lowered.

Why was she acting like this—avoiding eye contact, drawing away from him? It wasn't that she was over-whelmed by the fact he owned this place. The only other logical answer came to mind.

"I'm not trying to fob you off," he assured her. "These aren't payment or a pay-off for last night. I wanted us to spend the day here together."

He'd wanted her in that bed again tonight. And their time together didn't have to be over.

Why couldn't their connection continue back at the resort? He didn't know how long she was staying, but surely he would be able to wangle at least some quality time with her before he left on Monday.

His hands settled on her hips and he urged her close. "I have an idea. Move your things into my bungalow. You haven't been happy with Diamond Shores, but I'll do everything I can to fix that." His forehead tipped against hers and he grinned. "Our own private beach. The staff will treat you like a princess. There'll be hell to pay if they don't—"

"*No.*"

When she pulled away, the muscles in his gut wrenched. It was all he could do not to drag her back. Was it so important *where* they were?

Their kind of chemistry didn't rely on location. Even if important business was calling him away, they could still come together in the evening. After last night—the way she'd given herself so completely—Nina couldn't pretend she hadn't come to this island seeking a little one-on-one companionship. A fling hadn't figured on his agenda, but it had happened. No reason in the world that it couldn't continue a few more days yet.

But now she seemed determined to play hard to get.

"I want to go back." She lifted her eyes to meet his. "And I want to stay in my own room."

Her cool determination hit him in the chest. He bit down and did what he should have done sooner. He found her arm, brought her back, and held her firmly against him.

His gaze roamed her face as he spoke unforgivably near to her lips. "What about last night?"

He'd meant what he'd said. He'd never wanted to make love to anyone the way he'd wanted to make love to her. He hadn't been disappointed. She hadn't been either; he'd made sure of it. After her abandon, why the hard-to-get act now?

He held his breath.

Or had the act been last night?

Had this time away in the bush been nothing more than an adventure for a bored heiress?

She didn't answer his question. Rather the sparkle he loved to see in her eyes seemed to fade and die.

Gabriel's heart began to pound. He'd spoken to this woman about trust. About faith. And now, just like *that,* she wanted out?

She seemed about to say something more—something important. But then the resignation returned to her face and she put out her hand to accept the clothes. "I'll get changed and we can go."

He thought about her in those cut-offs…in his arms…in her prima-donna life away from here. He thought about how easily she was prepared to walk away, and a cold ball settled in the cradle of his stomach.

Setting his jaw, he handed over the clothes and, kicking himself for almost falling for a rich girl's games, stepped aside and let her pass.

CHAPTER SEVEN

NINA moved behind the curtain and changed into the stunning aqua one-piece and matching wrap Gabriel had brought back from the resort.

She ought to feel beautiful. Special. Instead she felt empty. She'd had such high hopes this morning about how this day would evolve, but in these last few minutes everything had soured.

Gabriel had knocked her for six with his admission that he owned this island. *Owned* it. She hadn't known Diamond Shores had changed hands since Alice had helped her get her job. In effect, Gabriel was her supreme boss; as well as the woman he wanted to sleep with, she was also one of the problems he needed to have removed. How on earth was she supposed to tell him that?

A few moments later they were tearing along the beach, the bike's engine roaring, the ocean waves crashing—and Gabriel's broad, obstinate back in her face. She was torn between needing to wean herself off the magnificent feel of him and desperately wanting to hold on tighter.

As they neared the tall blue side gates of the resort Gabriel changed down gears. When he skidded the bike to a stop, he averted his gaze while she alighted. Her feet on solid ground, she straightened the colourful wrap around her legs, and that empty feeling turned to flat-line hopelessness.

Gabriel Steele's mission here was to wipe out any rot. Given the many eyes and ears around Diamond Shores, her position wouldn't be a secret for long. Soon enough he'd hear about Nina Petrelle—her sub-standard performance, how the other staff disapproved of her breezy ticket in.

She didn't need to purge herself to him now. Tell him how she'd got to this place in her life. How she'd felt so displaced until he'd brought her back to life last night. He'd find out what he needed to know soon enough. Then it would only be a matter of time before she received her marching orders.

"Can you walk?" He dismounted the bike but kept his sunglasses in place. "I'll organise a motorised buggy if you're not sure of your ankle."

A sea breeze peeled through his dark hair, making it dance above the widow's peak, but his expression—or what she could see of it—remained unmoved. She hated his stiffness, that formal air. A few hours ago they'd talked and laughed and made the sweetest, and at other times wildest love. Now she had trouble imagining how the firm line of that mouth had pressed such tender af-fection upon her. The most beautiful time of her life was over.

"I'm fine to walk," she told him, determined to hold onto what remained of her dignity. "Thank you."

The mirrors of his glasses flashed in the sunlight as his head dipped a margin. "Can I make an appointment for our doctor to check out your leg and that bump on your head?"

"You've done enough."

Bittersweet longing ribboned around her heart. Yes, he'd done more than enough. He'd saved her life. She was standing here only because of this man's action and focus. That debt could never be repaid. If she felt gutted now, if she wished things could be different—that time could somehow rewind—she needed to remember she'd been given a second chance and go from there.

She headed off towards her quarters. Her vision had blurred and her heart was steadily sinking when that rich, deep voice came from behind her.

"Nina. Wait."

Her breath caught. After dashing a tear away, she spun back round. Sunglasses removed, he stood before her in those sexy jeans, his legs braced apart.

"I want you to have dinner with me tonight," he stated.

The unexpected thrill of having him follow her flashed brighter before it fizzled out. Dinner with Gabriel sounded like heaven, but any liaison was out of the question. When he found out who and *what* she was, he'd understand why.

"Gabriel, please—"

"I'm not taking no for an answer." He took both her hands in his, and the smile that made her melt sparkled up in his eyes. "You know it won't do any good to argue." When she squared her shoulders and stood her shaky ground, he shrugged. "I could always sweep you up and carry you off. It's worked before."

A laugh almost escaped.

From churlish to charming—and Gabriel's charming was so very hard to resist. But she had no choice. Now they were back at the resort, and their positions had changed so dramatically they couldn't go back to "last night."

She was working up another refusal when she spotted a woman in staff uniform gaping over at her: Tori Scribbins—Nina's roommate, and one of her few friends here. Tori's hand went theatrically to her heart and she pretended to faint. Nina's smile broke, and Gabriel's face slanted into her line of vision. With a precision movement he angled her, and next Nina knew she was shrieking with surprise, back in the cradle of those indomitable arms.

Her first instinct was to slap his shoulder, insist he let her down, but more powerful was the knowledge that he wasn't giving up on her. He never seemed to give up.

Maybe, just *maybe*…

Was it too stupid to hope again?

But she'd need to explain what was so difficult to put into words—how she'd come to be on this island, why she'd felt so lost—and she couldn't do that here. They needed privacy. She had a shift in the kitchen that ended at nine tonight. If she went to his bungalow after that…

He'd begun to stride off, but she pushed against his chest to pull him up.

"I'm busy till nine," she shot out.

His pace died while his crooked smile grew. "Which restaurant do you prefer?"

"Can we eat in? At your place?"

The sparkle in his eyes heated up. "It's a date."

Out the corner of her eye Nina spied Tori, leaning against the doorjamb of the room she must be cleaning; her jaw had dropped to the floor. She guessed this scene *would* look pretty remarkable…a strong, handsome, determined man whisking Nina the waitress away.

Tori was a true romantic. She'd be hearing wedding bells and planning honeymoons. Nina wouldn't presume to think that far ahead, but perhaps this rollercoaster Cinderella story might have some kind of happy ending after all.

Gabriel was saying, "Now I've got you, I might as well carry you to your room."

Her room was small and bare and in the staff quarters. No reason she couldn't get everything off her chest there—but no guarantee he would take the news well. Right or wrong, weak or strong, she wanted to hold onto hope as long as she could. Besides, she needed to get to her shift and he needed to get to work…

To his elimination plan.

"I don't want to be carried." But she smiled when she added, "And don't bother arguing this one. Put me down and I promise I'll see you after nine."

He studied her eyes, then reluctantly lowered her to her feet. He stole a lingering kiss from her cheek and murmured near her ear, "I'll have the champagne poured."

After she'd watched him stride away around a clump of pygmy date palms, Nina turned back to Tori, who was madly waving her over.

When Nina reached her roommate, Tori swept her into the suite and clapped the door shut.

Tori's coffee-coloured eyes were dancing with excitement. Her large watermelon wedge earrings swung as she clasped her hands under her chin and literally jumped up and down.

"When you didn't come in last night I didn't know what to think. I was going to call the alert if you weren't back by lunch. Now I understand why you went missing. My only question is…why are you back so soon? You should have called in a sickie."

Nine chewed her lip. She shouldn't blab. She didn't want to risk her secret leaking out before seeing Gabriel tonight. But she simply *had* to talk. She was bursting to spill about the first good thing to have happened to her in weeks.

They'd moved into the main room and now sat together on the massive semi-circular couch which faced a breathtaking view. The flutter in Nina's stomach beat faster as she told all about her fantastical evening—up to the point where her cliff-top angel had confessed his true identity as owner of the Diamond Shores Resort.

Tori slumped against the silk brocade cushions and held her cheeks. "Oh. My. Gosh. I'd have passed out. He *owns* the place? Everything?" Nina nodded and Tori tipped closer. "When are you going to see him again?"

"Tonight. After my shift."

"Are you going to tell him who you are before or after?"

"Before or after what?"

"He throws you down and ravages you, of course."

Nina's sucked down a breath. No use denying she wanted that to happen. A few minutes away from him seemed like an hour. An hour would seem like a week. By tonight she would be near ready to throw herself at him.

But she couldn't afford any more delays. The longer she kept her secret from Gabriel, the more chance he had of finding out the truth. It was better the news came from her.

"I'll tell him as soon as I get there."

They would either kiss, and the fun times would be on again, or he would not be amused and would refuse to contribute to delinquent behaviour as far as resort standards and reputation were concerned. Then again he *was* the boss. He could make *new* rules.

Sinking further into the couch, Tori draped her arms over her head and spoke to the rattan fan, circulating air around the vaulted wood beam ceiling. "I bet he kisses like a dream."

Nina recalled the sensation of Gabriel's lips covering hers…the way his mouth had coaxed her into sublime submission. "He kisses *better* than a dream."

He was drop-dead delectable. That body. That face. That creamy, dreamy voice.

"Maybe he has a brother you could introduce me to?" Tori pushed up and, sashaying over to her vacuum cleaner, gave her watermelon earring a sassy flick. "I could handle putting my duster out to pasture."

Nina was watching that earring swing. "You could get in trouble, wearing those." No jewellery was allowed other than studs and a watch. Mr Dorset, the general manager, was a stickler for dress code. Mr Dorset was a stickler for every rule.

Tori struck a pose oozing with attitude. "You're playing 'to the manner born' and *I* might get in trouble?"

The joke was that Nina *was* to the manner born. She hadn't appreciated the privileges she'd enjoyed growing up. She hadn't missed them when she'd had a well-paid job. Her life had seemed full. She'd been good at what she'd done. Her colleagues had respected her and vice versa.

Tori was deep in thought, fingering that earring. "If you ask me, management need to loosen up. *Don't be overly friendly with the guests,*" she sing-songed. *"Don't cough in public or we'll dock your pay."*

"You wouldn't be docked for coughing." Unless it was excessive.

Adjusting the vacuum head, Tori sent her a dry look. "This place needs a darn good shake-up. And you can tell your rich boyfriend that from me."

"He's not my boyfriend."

"Then what are you waiting for?" Tori stepped on the power, the vacuum roared to life, and she swung her hips in a hoola circle. "Work it, baby."

Promising to give Tori an update, either tomorrow or later that night, depending on how things went, Nina headed off to change. But she was preoccupied with hoping things would go well, buoyed by fond thoughts of her previous job back in Sydney. She'd belonged at *Shimmer* magazine in a way she would never belong here. One thing was certain. She needed to feel that sense of belonging again.

While dragging her uniform out from the single-door wardrobe, the phone extension caught Nina's eye. She'd asked the receptionist at *Shimmer* to keep her ear to the ground; sometimes management cut too many corners and people were needed back to fill the gaps. So why not take the initiative and call?

A moment later a voice Nina didn't recognise answered the connection in Sydney, and Nina cleared her throat. "Hello. Would Abbey King be there?"

"Abbey left last week. Can anyone else help?"

Nina's stomach bottomed out. Abbey was gone too? "Uh, I'm not sure who's there any more."

"May I ask who's speaking?"

"Nina Petrelle."

"And you're enquiring about…?"

"I used to work there."

The receptionist's tone changed, became low and flat. "*Shimmer* have no vacancies at this time."

Nina's hand fisted around the receiver as suffocating heat crept up her neck.

I was in charge of Features, she wanted to say. *I used to buy a latte with extra sprinkles every morning before work. I used to sit around the boardroom and discuss*

*upcoming stories and strategies with my colleagues. I
was part of that office, dammit!*

The receptionist's voice infiltrated the red haze.
"Hello? Were you calling about a job?"

Nina set her teeth. "I already *have* a job."

She slammed the receiver down.

Don't cry. Don't you dare cry.

If she started she might not be able to stop, because
that same draining question was whispering again in her
mind…

Who are you? Where will you end up?

She knew she would survive. It was just a matter of
staying strong.

But if Gabriel threw her out tonight she didn't know
what she'd do.

With a spring in his step, Gabriel headed down the
wide slate path, which was lined by a jungle of lush
tropical garden. Unwilling to admit defeat, he'd made
a no-holds-barred play to see Nina again and she'd ac-
quiesced. He wasn't prepared to throw in the towel
without at least writing a closing chapter to their beach-
side affair.

When he'd told her that he owned this island resort
initially he'd thought she was embarrassed. Then he'd
thought she was being a princess, and then he'd surmised
that he'd merely lost his appeal. But when she'd walked
away, resigned yet also somehow brave, he'd known
something more lay behind her change in attitude.

He remembered their conversation the previous
night…the way she'd opened up.

What had knocked the wind out of her? he wondered. She'd said she wanted to know who she was.
He'd blamed her general dislike of the resort on service

and facilities, but after seeing how bereft she'd looked before he'd called her back, he knew it went deeper than that. The obstacle, the crisis bringing her down, was waiting for her here.

Something dug into his hip. He reached and pulled a shell from his pocket. Before leaving this morning he'd found it on the bathroom shelf. Knowing Nina must have left it there, on impulse he'd taken it with him. He focused on the shell's decorative rays and remembered Nina's incredible smile.

He held the shell tighter.

He wouldn't rest until A: he found out all of Nina's story, and B: he fixed whatever was wrong. If she needed an ally, no matter how busy he got here, he'd be it.

"Excuse me, Mr Steele?"

Gabe wheeled around. Horace Dorset, General Manager of Diamond Shores Resort, was striding up the path. Dorset, with a lemon rosebud adorning his lapel, gave him a pleasant, enquiring look. "Everything well with you, sir?"

"I received your message," said Gabe. Dorset wanted to speak with him about standardising staff prerequisites. Good plan, but not now. "I'll get back to you tomorrow."

Dorset nodded, but didn't bow off. "I see you've introduced yourself to some of the staff."

Gabriel cast his mind back. "No. Only the managers."

"The young lady…?"

Young lady? He meant Nina?

Gabriel laughed. "You're mistaken. Nina's a guest." Dorset's brows slanted, then he shook his head. "You're confusing her with someone else,' Gabriel pointed out. Although he wasn't sure how anyone could mistake an air that confirmed an impeccable upbringing…the way she held herself…the way she spoke.

Dorset thought she was staff? Absurd.

And yet Dorset kept looking at him with something like pity pinching his brows.

Gabriel thought more, then waved an impatient arm towards the hotel. "I saw her go into her room, for God's sake."

"Not *her* room, Mr Steele. A housekeeping trolley was outside. Perhaps Nina entered to help another staff member clean."

Gabriel probed Dorset's cool gaze. If Dorset thought this was funny, he wasn't laughing. "What the hell are you talking about?"

"The woman you saw is a waitress. Nina Petrelle started with Diamond Shores six weeks ago." Dorset's shoulders rolled back. "We like to pride ourselves on our standards, and I'm afraid Nina has made one too many errors. I've been patient so far, but this episode, withholding her identity from a guest—from *you*, Mr Steele—is an infringement that cannot be ignored. Measures must be taken."

Gabriel's mind felt frozen. He opened his palm and glared at the shell. Had he heard her name right?

"The staff are well aware of our number one rule," Dorset continued. "No fraternising with guests. I want you to know I'm very strict on that. It can be tempting for a single young woman to covet what others here enjoy—"

Gabriel shot up a hand. He was interested in only one thing. "What did you say her name was?"

"Nina."

"Last name?"

"Petrelle."

Nina Petrelle. Anthony Petrelle's baby sister?

A thousand memories flashed through his mind— playing touch in the Petrelles' enormous manicured backyard...surfing at Bondi that last summer... Anthony's sister, that right little madam, sticking it to him every chance she got. If she wasn't jeering at his favourite shoes, she was niggling about his numerous after-school jobs, or insisting he should do them all a favour and buy a new pair of glasses.

She'd been the kind of over-indulged kid who had a tantrum if no one noticed the new designer ribbon in her silky blonde hair. Nina Petrelle had been *the* poster girl for spoilt rotten. But for the sake of his friendship with Anthony, who'd been as down to earth as the next bloke, he'd kept his mouth shut.

Gabriel shook his brain and came back to the present.

How the tables had turned. When he'd known Nina last his surname had been Turner, his mother's name. But if Nina didn't recognise him, he sure as hell hadn't recognised her. For one, she was twice the size—and in all the right places. Her hair was six shades darker too.

He remembered her body writhing beneath him in the firelight last night and his insides twisted.

He'd made love to Nina Petrelle?

Dorset's voice cut into his thoughts. "Mr Steele, I apologise for her behaviour. Gold-digging will not be tolerated here. I'll go speak with her now."

As Dorset moved off, Gabriel gripped the older man's forearm. His tone was close to dangerous. "I don't want you to say or do a thing with regard to Miss Petrelle."

"I—I beg your pardon—?"

"You heard me." He released Dorset's arm. "I'll handle this."

Dorset opened his mouth to protest, but when Gabriel glowered Dorset nodded, although clearly unhappy with the decision. "As you wish."

Gabriel continued on to his accommodation, the shell tucked inside one clenched hand. He felt as if his chest had been rammed by a tree trunk.

Yes, when she'd told him her name he'd thought twice, but she looked nothing like the squirt who'd hung around and annoyed the crap out of him all those years ago. What was she doing working here? Her family was loaded.

Perhaps they'd had a falling out? She obviously needed money—badly enough to hunt down and snare herself a millionaire. Although her near drowning must have been an accident; no one would risk their life that way. But clearly she'd taken advantage of the situation from there, playing him with a combination of coy and sassy to see which stoked his fires best.

Let someone have faith in you again, she'd said. Hell, he'd really thought she'd cared.

He kicked open his front door.

What a schmuck!

As he stood in the foyer of his bungalow, another thought sprang to mind.

Nina knew he owned this island, but she didn't know who he was—or rather who he'd been: Gabe Turner, her brother's egghead friend, the "pauper" she'd lived to humiliate. The guy who'd kept his lip buttoned while she tried to put him in his place.

Gabriel's smile was more a sneer.

He couldn't wait to see her face when she found out. But a greater challenge awaited her. Not only was

Nina a down-on-her-luck gold-digger, according to Dorset she was no good at her job. How on earth had she got a position here in the first place?

But the bigger question was…

He dropped the shell and ground it beneath his heel. *How soon could he get rid of her?*

FREE BOOKS OFFER

To get you started, we'll send you
2 FREE books and a FREE gift

There's no catch, everything is **FREE**

Accepting your 2 **FREE** books and **FREE** mystery gift
places you under no obligation to buy anything.

Be part of the Mills & Boon® Book Club™ and receive your favourite
Series books up to 2 months before they are in the shops and delivered
straight to your door. Plus, enjoy a wide range of **EXCLUSIVE** benefits!

- Best new women's fiction – delivered right to
  your door with FREE P&P

- Avoid disappointment – get your books up to
  2 months before they are in the shops

- No contract – no obligation to buy

We hope that after receiving your free books you'll
want to remain a member. But the choice is yours.
So why not give us a go? You'll be glad you did!

Visit **millsandboon.co.uk** to stay up to date
with offers and to sign-up for our newsletter

2 **FREE** books
and a
FREE gift

POCIA

Mrs/Miss/Ms/Mr   Initials

BLOCK CAPITALS PLEASE

Surname

Address

Postcode

Email

MILLS & BOON®

NO STAMP NEEDED!

⊛ MILLS & BOON®
Book Club
FREE BOOK OFFER
FREEPOST NAT 10298
RICHMOND
TW9 1BR

NO STAMP
NECESSARY
IF POSTED IN
THE U.K. OR N.I.

CHAPTER EIGHT

AFTER her shift in the kitchen, Nina showered, slipped into a light summer dress, and made her way to Gabriel Steele's ultra-private bungalow. Her throat was tight with nerves and her stomach was riding a rollercoaster by the time she dropped the knocker on the imposing double doors. After several moments, when no one answered, she dared to turn the handle and ease inside.

Towering potted palms, mirror-polished marble counters, exquisitely crafted teak furniture, fresh sprays of exotic flowers... Surrounded by such luxury, in "guest" versus "employee" mode, she felt the dizzy scent of excess fill her head.

Spending last night with Gabriel in that cabin had been like a beautiful elixir, a once-in-a-lifetime experience which would live for ever in her mind and her heart. Being here in this setting, about to be with Gabriel again, was possibly an even headier thrill. After spending hours packing dishwashers, the sight of that cushiony white couch was almost enough to convince her that indulgence—this kind of over-the-top lavish extravagance—wasn't so offensive after all. She would love to lie back on the couch and put her feet up.

Massaging the weary small of her spine, she did

another sweep of the main room. Gabriel wasn't here. Limping slightly, she edged towards the opened concertina doors.

The full moon spilled a shimmering river of gold across an otherwise black sea. The scent of salt and natural floral perfumes filled the warm air, and on the deck Gabriel stood with a phone pressed to his ear. He wore dark tailored trousers and a crisp white Oxford shirt. His sleeves were rolled to below the elbow, leaving tanned corded forearms exposed. His dark hair was freshly showered, wet and stylishly messy.

The overall picture—complete with a vee of wiry hair visible at his throat and broad shoulders adorned in silk weave—was enough for Nina to clutch at her fast-beating heart. She hadn't thought he could be more attractive than when she'd first seen him—muscles pumped and bare chest battle-whipped.

She'd been wrong.

Without trying, he dominated any scene.

Angling around, Gabriel spotted her. He nodded twice into the phone, gave a parting remark, then disconnected and moved towards her.

"Important call?" she asked, when she might easily have said, *The sight of you turns my legs to jelly.*

"My second in charge," he said, sauntering nearer. "Zane Rutley knows as much about my company as I do, but he likes to keep me up to date. Says there's no rest for the wicked."

"You've known him long?"

"Since university. We duxed Management Accounting and Strategy."

"Ooh, bad boys."

He grinned. "I can't speak for Zane."

She didn't know about Zane Rutley either, but

Gabriel Steele could make any woman melt at a hundred paces. His every move was measured, exact, and at the same time effected with inherent masculine grace. Her cheeks heated. Although he hadn't touched her yet, she was already simmering inside.

When he stopped before her, she expected his mouth to break into his trademark sexy-as-sin smile. She expected him to sweep her up and kiss her as he'd kissed her through the magical hours of last night. But his lopsided grin remained fixed, and the gleam in his eye seemed somehow…cool.

She felt a little off balance when his fingers curled around her arm and his freshly shaved cheek rubbed lightly against hers.

His lips brushed her temple. "How was your afternoon?"

"Busy." Her ankle throbbed to punctuate the point.

He drew away and assessed her butter-yellow dress, his gaze deliberately trailing her shape in a vaguely predatory fashion before he ushered her, a hand on her elbow, towards the outdoor setting.

He indicated an ice bucket. "Champagne?"

"You said you'd have it poured," she teased.

"Nothing worse than when bubbles go flat."

He popped the cork, and foam spilled over the rim to darken the timber near his feet. To take her mind off his intoxicating sandalwood scent, she inspected the champagne label.

"My father used to keep a couple of bottles of that for special occasions."

"It's a rare vintage." He handed her a glass. "Is your father here with you on the island?"

The breath went out of her. "He died a few years ago."

His gaze jumped up from his pouring of a second glass. His searching eyes clouded and his voice dropped. "Nina…I'm sorry."

She sighed quietly. Gabriel could be so strong, yet there were times, like now, he could be so sensitive. As if he truly knew her. Knew her like no one else could.

But then he cleared his throat, raised his glass to his lips, and the deeper moment was gone.

"I bumped into someone this afternoon." He sipped, swallowed. "He told me the most fascinating story."

He was watching her over the rim of his glass and the glint in his eyes now seemed almost steely. She'd seen a few sides to Gabriel—uncompromising hero, charmer, believer, lover. When they'd left the cabin this morning he'd been cagey. But the vibes she caught now didn't fit with any of that.

That pointed gleam in his gaze was enough to make her shiver. Who was the "someone" he'd spoken with?

She sipped champagne without tasting it and when he didn't divulge more she asked, "What did this man say?"

A humourless smile tugged one side of his mouth. "I thought you might like to tell me."

Her breath died in her chest. She closed her eyes as her stomach rolled over twice, then sank to her knees. Her throat convulsed and she swallowed.

"You know."

His chin went up. "I know."

She'd been caught out before she'd had the chance to come clean. Someone had let on that she was an employee of the island and, given the hard line of his jaw, Gabriel wasn't pleased.

She managed to keep her voice steady. "Gabriel, let me explain—"

"I will. But first…"

His palm scooped behind her neck and his mouth opened over hers. The lip-to-lip contact sent jets of recognition shooting through her veins. Every cell in her body seemed to tremble, light up and press in. The renewed awareness was so strong, so vital, it was all she could do to remember that…

That this kiss was different.

Rougher.

Dominating.

When their lips parted, her world had slanted and the room seemed to spin. A pulse beat wildly in his cheek, and if he released her there was every possibility she might slide to the floor. As if reading her thoughts, he dragged out a chair. Numbness taking over, she fell into the seat.

"I took the liberty of ordering," he told her, gesturing to the silver domes set on the table while her mind whirled on. He lifted one dome and the aroma of lobster mornay, scalloped potatoes and buttered asparagus filled her lungs.

He folded into the adjacent slat-backed chair.

"Before you tell your story, Nina, I thought you might like to know more about mine." He removed his dome, then his napkin flicked out with a *snap*. "I became aware that Diamond Shores' previous owner was interested in a buy-out when I paid for April's wedding and reception. She has no family. After her dedication to her job these past five years, that gift was the least I could do." He nodded amicably at her plate. "Eat before it gets cold."

Her limbs were fifty-pound weights. Her lips and tongue were rubber.

"I…I'm not very hungry."

He collected his cutlery and continued his thread.

"You know the resort is running at a loss," he said, in a monotone that still managed to send heatwaves shimmering over her skin. "The hand-over was low-key. Making my presence known here only to the managers was a strategic decision. It's difficult to get an accurate idea of performance when fanfares announce your every move. I needed a clear indication of which heads should roll."

His gaze, holding hers, was both ablaze and cold as a snowstorm. An arctic chill chased up her spine. She couldn't bear the stomach knots a moment longer.

"I was features editor for a teen magazine," she got out, clenching the napkin beside her plate. "I was retrenched along with others. I needed a job, but there was nothing available in publishing. It was all I knew."

All she was.

"That was your crisis?" he surmised, and she nodded. His napkin patted one corner of his mouth. "How did you get a job here?"

"A friend's father knew the owner. The former owner." Or so it seemed.

"You had no experience?"

"Next to none."

His short laugh was abrasive. "No wonder the place is sinking."

She set her teeth, but continued, "Alice said the hours would be long but the money was good. I could make my mortgage repayments." Blindly studying her plate, she leaned back. "I didn't want to lose my house."

When she levelled her gaze at him, something almost human flashed across his face. But then he took a mouthful of champagne and placed the glass down heavily.

"And yesterday?"

"Was my first afternoon off in what seemed like for ever," she said. "I was physically and emotionally drained. Most of the staff don't like me, you see. And it's true I have a lot to learn. They have every right to feel undervalued. That doesn't help the way I feel." Lonely. Very nearly hopeless. "Yesterday I wanted to get as far away from the resort as I could. I started walking, collecting shells to send to my baby nephew back in Sydney."

"Nephew?"

"My sister's baby. Codie's six months old. Jill's a single mum. She deferred her Masters in Biology to look after him for the first couple of years and—" She stopped, sighed. "You're really not interested in any of that, are you?"

Gabriel held his impassive face. She was a consummate manipulator, trying to find his vulnerable spot even now. Years had passed, but nothing had changed. Nina was used to getting what she wanted, and it seemed she wanted his sympathy. Wanted him to bail her out.

This afternoon, when he'd uncovered her game, his chest had filled with rage. Having known the princess fourteen-year-old Nina Petrelle had been, he'd easily joined the dots. He had no idea where the Petrelle fortune had gone, but the woman sitting across from him, trying to tug at his heartstrings, needed money badly enough to don an apron. She'd lucked out when he'd come bounding along yesterday to save her. She'd played her cards well and he'd fallen for her.

To a degree.

He didn't like to be deceived. He'd envisaged sacking her on the spot, throwing her out of her lodgings. He'd imagined the crocodile tears, her pleas, those attempts to use her *femme fatale* skills to get her way. In hindsight he believed only one thing she'd said.

She wanted to find herself—aka needed to have, to hold, real money again.

His money.

His lips stretched over his teeth.

Time for Act II.

"You might recall I said I'd known a Nina once." He collected his cutlery again and cut into firm asparagus. "Tell me, have you ever known anyone else called Gabriel?"

His comment pulled Nina up. Her nape prickled with a different kind of awareness as she nodded. "A friend of my brother's. Gabe Turner."

"What else do you remember?"

"He was a stuffed-shirt geek who my brother, for some reason, adored." That horrid gnawing in her gut deepened. She studied the man sitting opposite and instinctively sat back. "Why do you want to know?"

His ice-blue gaze held hers for an endless moment before he announced, "Because that Gabe is this Gabe. Gabriel Turner is me."

Nina wanted to throw back her head and laugh. She'd never heard anything so ridiculous. Instead she paused to consider the statement more deeply.

"No," she groaned, slowly shaking her head. "You said…your name is *Steele.*"

But from the start hadn't there been a distant whisper of this? Seeing him standing on that cliff a second before she'd passed out…even then he'd seemed somehow familiar. This man—the man she'd shared a bed with— he couldn't possibly be that stiff, zero taste, no personality dweeb she remembered from all those years ago.

Could he?

"Turner was my mother's name," he said. "My aunt's name. When I made amends with my father in my late teens, I took his name. Steele."

She snapped shut her hanging jaw. "But those ugly sun-sensitive glasses?"

"Laser surgery."

"Your hair?"

"Comb-overs were never in."

"You look…taller."

"I grew."

"You're *rich.*"

He grinned. "Yes, I am."

She studied his face again, and every molecule of oxygen seeped from her lungs.

Oh, God. It was true.

Her fingers started to tingle and her heart began to pound. She needed a paper bag before she hyperventilated and passed out.

"Faith, my aunt, passed away five years ago from a stroke," he said, colouring in the rest. "My father died from a coronary not long after we met."

Her vision clouded and tunnelled in. Aunt Faith… yes, she remembered. His story fitted, but her brain was too overloaded to offer condolences.

As a thousand memories rained down in a battering gale, she peered into Gabe's hard gaze and somehow managed to set her priorities straight. Not having seen her for well over a decade, Gabe Turner had shown up out of the blue and saved her life?

It was magical thinking, but she wondered whether her brother had had a hand in his buddy being in the right place at the right time. Anthony had always looked out for her in a cool, big-brother kind of way. She only wished someone had been there to look out for him when he'd needed it.

Her brow tingled.

Last night Gabriel had said he'd lost someone close. Someone who'd had faith in him when he'd had little in himself. Anthony.

An image dawned—a clear snapshot of her brother's face—and despite the situation Nina's mouth twitched. The image zoomed in to show Anthony's confounded expression and a smile twitched again.

Gabriel pushed his plate aside. "You think this is funny?"

"Can you imagine what Anthony would say if he knew? He'd be thinking what a huge joke this was on us both. Gabe Turner hated me, I hated Gabe Turner more, and Anthony...well, he loved us both."

She'd hated the way Gabe Turner had ignored her. Hated those revolting glasses. Hated the fact that his clothes were dull from too many washes and yet he still filled out trousers better than any boy she'd known. Worse, while he'd struggled to afford new socks, he'd always held his head so high. As if he was better than everyone else. Certainly better than her.

Now Gabe Turner was a wealthy man of the world. A gorgeous multimillionaire with whom she'd made love until both were so spent neither could draw another breath.

Her stomach double-flipped.

Her and Geeky Gabe. How totally weird was that?

She must have been staring at him because he pulled in his chin. "What?"

"Don't you want to know?"

"Know what?"

"Why, when my family was so wealthy, I'm waitressing now."

His gaze skimmed her lips, his jaw flexed, then he crossed his arms over that big delectable chest. "That question had crossed my mind."

She was happy to answer. There happened to be a question he might be able to answer for her in return.

"Anthony's death really shook my parents up," she told him. "Me and Jill too, but we were young enough not to understand the full weight of the situation. That Anthony really wasn't coming home and our lives would never be the same. He'd been the jewel in the crown of our family. Everyone loved Anthony. For a long time no one could accept he was gone."

Gabriel's arms slowly unravelled. "It was a tragic accident."

"He loved speed and the idea of taking chances, pushing the limits." Anthony had skinned his elbows and knees more than once shooting the bowl on his skateboard. "He said he was either going into the air force or to work for National Security as a secret agent."

A distant smile shone in Gabriel's eyes. "He'd have done it too. He had the smarts as well as the guts."

The question burned on the tip of her tongue. She'd wanted to know for such a long time, only she hadn't thought anyone would know—not even her father, who'd loved Anthony better than anyone. But Gabe and her brother had been so close.

"Anthony must have known he couldn't possibly do it," she murmured. "Not in the dead of night. The fact that the place was cursed would've been enough to keep *me* away." She cast Gabriel—Gabe—an imploring look over the candlelit table. "Did he talk to you about going there?"

Maintaining a thousand-yard stare past her shoulder, he slanted his head and finally nodded.

Nina's attention picked up, but rather than sharing, Gabriel only thinned the line of his mouth.

"We knew it was some kind of a dare," she prodded. "I heard my parents talking about Roger someone."

"Roger Maxwell."

"That's it. He dared Anthony to scale the north face of Mount Spectre near your school. It had something to do with a girl Anthony liked."

"Roger started ribbing Anthony in front of her," said Gabe, in a low, gravelled tone. "Saying he was a wimp, a chicken, which was the most idiotic thing I'd ever heard. When Anthony laughed it off and went to walk away Roger challenged him. It was only because Roger liked this girl too, and Anthony knew it. Anthony laughed again—until the girl asked whether he was afraid of the curse."

Nina remembered. "A jilted lover was supposed to have jumped to his death there a hundred years ago. He became a ghost who guarded the peak and gave anyone who climbed such a fright that they'd rather fall to their death than face him."

"Anthony wanted a trial run up the cliffside first," he said. "Without Roger and the others looking on."

"I can't believe he risked his life to impress a girl."

"He wanted me to come along."

What? She sat forward. "You were there? My parents didn't ever tell me."

His jaw clenched. "I told him the only way I'd go was if I could manage to catch him when he fell. I knew he could be stubborn, but I didn't think he'd try it. I was so angry with him." He blinked and his voice deepened. "Angrier with myself."

She knew how Gabriel felt...somehow responsible... wanting to rework history. She'd wanted to be there for

Anthony too, to convince him not to be so foolish, and all for the sake of a bet. But no amount of wishing or blame would bring her brother back.

"He made the decision to climb that rock," she assured Gabriel now. "No one else."

His eyes burned into space. "I was his best friend. I should've talked him out of it. Or physically held him back."

The way he'd physically held *her* back yesterday, when he'd dragged her out of the surf and she'd refused to listen to sound advice? She'd thought at the time he was being bossy, but he'd only had her best interests at heart when he'd made sure she'd lain still in case of concussion. All those years ago when she'd hated him—or thought she had—she'd recognised that strength in him too.

Natural. Unswerving.

In her mind she saw Gabriel standing on the very edge of that cliff, the wind gusting through his hair and opened shirt, as if he was daring the gods to force him off. Her gaze roamed the lines of his face and understanding crept in. Now she knew who he was, how their pasts were connected, it seemed obvious.

"You were thinking about my brother yesterday, weren't you?"

One dark eyebrow arched and he leant back. "I didn't set out to climb to the island's highest point. Heights and I don't mix well. I'd had a quiet, uneventful bushwalk in mind, to clear my mind before heading back to the cabin." His gaze dropped and he reached for his glass. "Then you happened along."

She fought the urge to reach over and touch his hand. "Anthony would've been so proud if he'd seen you dashing to my rescue."

His eyes snapped up, but then a shadow of a smile

hovered at the corners of his mouth. His gaze held hers, and as the moment wound down the space between them seemed to thrum with a different, deeper meaning.

But then he sucked back a breath and shoved to his feet. Glaring at the dark rolling sea, he drove a hand through his hair, then set his fists low on his hips. "None of that makes any difference."

"Any difference to what?"

He faced her. "Nina, you can't stay."

Air seeped from her lungs. The present and its challenges rose up again and she slumped.

"You're sacking me." Not a question. Rather a flat-line statement.

What had she expected? A reunion with balloons and a rendition of "Auld Lang Syne"? Bottom line: no matter what vow she'd made to improve, she was a less than competent waitress, and those who didn't perform must be eliminated.

Regardless of the way they'd made love last night, this evening it was *Goodbye, Nina*.

Gabriel turned back to face the ocean, wringing his hands on the rail.

He'd had the scenario worked out. Announce that he knew her identity, then slap her with the final slam-dunk details of his own. Nina had deceived him. Dorset must have thought him a fool to fall for her act. No one manipulated him the way she had and got away with it— particularly when *this* Nina was the obnoxious teen who years ago had rattled his cage any chance she'd got.

And yet—

Dropping his chin, Gabriel clenched the rail and let out a quiet groan.

After speaking about Anthony, he could practically hear his best mate demanding he do something to help his little sister, and do it now. No matter how much he might want to, he couldn't and wouldn't ignore it. Anthony had been too good a friend. God knew why he'd befriended him, the geek, but Gabriel would never forget it.

But throwing money at Nina didn't seem right. He'd never taken charity; Anthony wouldn't have wanted hand-outs either. If Nina was hoping for a signed blank cheque—sorry, not happening.

Keeping her on here was out of the question too. Turning this place around depended on sticking to the narrow but profitable road. Not even Anthony's memory could influence him to jeopardise that success.

There was only one solution. For Anthony's sake—for the sake of what he and Nina had shared last night—he would help find her more suitable employment. Somewhere she could shine, find herself again. And if she gave him any cheek about it…

His mind made up, he angled back. "I have contacts in the industry."

She dragged her gaze from her untouched plate. "What industry?"

"Publishing. I'll set up an interview or two in Sydney."

Her eyes widened and she pushed to her feet. Her mouth worked soundlessly before she breathed out, "You'd do that for me?"

She could be near her sister and nephew, earn decent money. Keep her home. All she had to do was take a job which would be created after he pulled a few strings and stay the hell out of his life. His head—his pride—had been messed with enough.

But she was sighing and shaking her head. "I'm sorry. I can't let you do that."

His temper spiked. "Why the hell not?"

"I can't accept a job I haven't won on my own merit."

Well, she'd done it before, to get her job here. And sleeping with a rich stranger to get a leg up apparently wasn't taboo either.

He leaned back against the rail and slid his hands into his trouser pockets. "Off nepotism? That's very noble."

"Not noble. I've learned my lesson. Next time I move on, it'll be to something I've earned."

His eyes narrowed on hers. She was playing him again, and, *damn,* she was good at it.

"Let me put it this way," he said. "You need a job, a job that you know, and I insist on helping you make that happen."

Her lips pressed together. "No."

He withdrew his hands from his pockets. "Not even if it'll get you back home to your family? I thought you wanted to rediscover yourself—you can't do that here."

"You're right. I can't. Not completely. But I have to believe that my reputation and credentials will get me the right job at the right time. I don't know that I'd ever be able to gain the respect of the staff here. I won't make that mistake twice. I won't jump the queue and take on something I don't deserve."

He stopped less than an arm's length away, and instantly the space between them crackled with heat. Despite their disagreeable past, and the battlefield they occupied now, the grooves in his mind slotted back into blistering memories of last night and the undeniable force that clawed at him whenever she was near.

He set his jaw. Got a grip. Slapped that mental wall back up.

"Nina, you can't continue to work here."

Her slim nostrils flared before she slowly nodded. "I understand. I do." She glanced over their cold meals. "If it's all the same with you, I won't stay for dessert."

She turned, and even as his throat and chest burned he noticed her limp as she walked through into the main room.

And don't bother with the lame act to get sympathy either, he wanted to call after her. He wasn't that much of a sucker.

But when the limp seemed to get worse, the further she walked, Gabriel scrubbed his jaw.

Working all afternoon and half the night, she must have been on her feet the whole time. From Mr Dorset's account, Nina would know she didn't have another card up her sleeve; she couldn't call in sick or beg off early. Had the doctor even checked her out? Gabriel would bet not.

He dragged his hand down his face, tried to come up with another way. Then, cursing under his breath, he strode off to catch her up. This woman would drive him *nuts.*

"For God's sake, Nina, come back and sit down."

The way she was going she'd only cause herself more harm.

When she kept walking Anthony's shadow breathed down Gabriel's neck, and the voice in his head—over his shoulder—grew louder.

Stop her. Make her listen. She's hurt. She's my sister and she needs your help!

Gabriel put some steel in his voice. *"Nina."*

"I'm going."

"Going where?"

She angled back. "I'm looking forward to finding out."

She was so stubborn. So annoying, and so...amazingly attractive. As her eyes glistened into his, his heartbeat boomed in his ears and he knew to his soul what had to be done.

The pull—this fierce physical attraction—was too strong to ignore. No matter how many times she walked away, he would have to bring her back because what he'd tried to block from his mind all the long day *would* happen. He knew it as well as he knew his own name. They *would* make love again and she'd better prepare herself.

The way he was feeling, last night had only been practice.

CHAPTER NINE

GABRIEL strode over and drew her body hard against his. As his mouth came crashing down upon hers, Nina braced herself not to weaken.

In a way, she'd expected this. This man's middle name might be "irresistible," but after that discussion she would rather jump from a plane without a parachute than confirm the terrible, wonderful heat his kiss stirred deep inside her.

He wanted her gone. No problem.

She was going.

Go…ing…

After several breathtaking, ultra-persuasive moments, the kiss softly broke and Gabriel's hot-lidded gaze brushed over her face. His fingertips traced hair from her brow and he murmured, "Are you listening now?"

She swallowed, but held her chin high. "No."

He kissed her again, and those defences crumbled more. Her head told her to pull back, to slap his face; who did he think he was, assaulting her like this? Her body, on the other hand, whispered to her heart to press in more.

His kisses only got better.

When his lips left hers a second time, her breathing was tellingly deep. A practised hand skimmed her side before he took a lingering kiss from her temple, her cheek. To stop herself from snaking her arms around his neck, she fisted his shirt in her hands.

Feeling giddy, she groaned, "What do you want from me?"

He cupped her chin. "You have to ask?"

She closed her eyes and prayed. She had to clear her foggy brain. Had to keep smart. Keep strong.

"You're Gabe Turner," she reminded herself. "You *sacked* me." Her eyes opened. "If you think I'll sleep with you again, you've got rocks in your head."

He scooped her up into his arms and began to walk.

She managed to straighten to a board as her stomach pitched. "I'll scream."

His mouth hooked into the sexiest of smiles. "Promise?"

As he carried her into his bedroom, Nina told herself she should struggle and demand he set her down. She had to put this rabid sexual thirst away. Lock the door and throw away the double-edged key. Because, while this might seem a natural extension of their previous smouldering night together, tomorrow she would pay the price.

She'd already lost her job. She didn't want to lose her self-respect too.

But by the time he stopped in the middle of the shadowy bedroom, and she gazed up into those haunting ice-blue eyes, her arguments had wound down to nought. Rather than warnings she heard only a sweet chorus, urging her to go forward. It was as if history were already written. The deed was already done. Right or wrong, she would go through with this. The reason was simple.

There'd never be another Gabriel. One more time with him would be more than a lifetime with anyone else.

As if he read her thoughts, the lines either side of his eyes crinkled with a soft smile. He crossed the room and set her carefully down beside the bed. Then he flicked down the quilt and stood back, running an eye over her dress, as if approving of the design but also analysing the most effective way to remove it.

Stepping close again, he gripped the hem and the dress slid like butter up over her hips, her waist, her head, finally her arms. While she trembled inside from crown to toe, his hot gaze consumed her. She felt every stroke of his appraisal as it sizzled over her strapless bra, lower, to her abdomen then across her red silk briefs.

His gaze jumped and held hers again while he peeled the shirt off his back and dropped it to the timber floor. With the broad expanse of his chest rising and falling, he pulled her up against his hard heat and, after murmuring that he'd wanted her all day, claimed her mouth with his again.

She'd expected his kiss to ignite her as it had last night, to take over her senses and leave her deliciously weak and desperately wanting. She'd expected the same fireworks to leap up, lighting her blood until flames devoured any lingering whim to resist.

She was surprised.

When they'd lain together last night she'd never felt more alive, more grateful for each breath, and for the man who'd made another day possible. Tonight his kiss went beyond that. This heady emotion wasn't about outside influence or circumstance. It was about them… how well they meshed…how amazingly well they fitted. As his head angled more, and he kissed her thoroughly, her soul floated away and joined his, twining and spiralling off into blessed infinity.

Nina coiled her arms around his neck, unable to imagine anyone feeling as much as she felt at that moment. The desire was both an all-consuming necessity and a magnificent release that remade her, as light as the moonbeams slanting in through the open plantation blinds. No one could ever have felt this deeply before this.

Before them.

His mouth gradually broke from hers to trail down the side of her throat. She arched her neck, allowing him better access, and sighed when he snapped open her bra. As the bra dropped between them, his mouth slid along her collarbone and, one palm supporting her weight, he lowered her back upon the sheets.

He unzipped his trousers and not soon enough stood before her naked. She shouldn't stare. She'd seen him *sans* clothes before. The straight stance, lean hips, hard bronzed frame that tapered into a perfect V. This sight proved yet again that he was no ordinary man. He was so much more than that.

He rested one knee on the bed and, with his hands either side of her shoulders, asked, "You okay? Your ankle?"

Relishing the abandon, she dragged him down. "I'm not thinking about my foot."

While she battled to keep her heart behind her ribs, his palm traced down over her waist, her leg, all the way to her bandage and then up again. Above the knee, however, his direction curled in to feather up her inner thigh. When his fingertips skimmed her panties' damp crotch a flash of darkest desire plunged through her, gripping her insides and coating them with warm liquid want.

Biting her lip, she turned her head towards the pillow. "You want to torture me?"

He chuckled. "Not the word I'd have used."

She found his hand and held his palm against the pulse that was both freeing her spirit as well as compressing every thought and feeling gloriously tight. His lips nuzzling hers, he tugged her panties' crotch aside. At the same time as cool air brushed between her thighs, his mouth left hers. A moment later his warm breath was a whisper away from her most intimate, private place.

Gripping the sheet at her sides, she fought the urge to buck her hips, to let him know how dearly she wanted this. Wanted him. When he urged her folds apart, and his tongue dipped to swirl over the sensitive nub, she bit her lip harder to quell the cry.

"You're beautiful," he said.

Then he kissed her again, with his lips, with his tongue, twirling and tasting until he'd drawn out every ounce of vulnerability she'd ever hidden from the world. She felt the roughness of his beard and the pleasure in his smile as he groaned and hummed against her. The vibration filtered through her blood, igniting a glittering roadmap of longing that swept along her veins. And then…

One second she was vaguely aware of her surroundings, of her individual heartbeat and the rhythmic wash of the waves outside. The next the spiral of sensation had smashed through the ceiling. The tingling burn heightened, deepened, widened, until nothing existed but the heat-lightning rushing over her breasts, scorching her nipples and shooting blazing stars through her mind to her core.

From the moment Nina surrendered, Gabriel knew tonight wouldn't be their last. Holding her now, as she cried out his name, he was struck by another revelation. Whatever lay behind their fiery connection, it was real—and she knew it too. She wanted this to continue as much as he did—if not more.

As her contractions eased, and she breathed out a full-bodied sigh, he pulled himself up over her amazing curves. Her eyes were closed and an almost innocent smile graced her swollen lips. He drank in the sight, drawing out the anticipation, and with every passing second his want for her grew.

Dreamy, she blinked open her eyes. She focused, then her smile fanned and her arms went out to him.

Pressing tender kisses to her brow, he entered her, with finite, together-again care. When he was certain she was ready, when he felt her urgency had built again to breaking point, he gripped the top of the bedhead with one hand and cupped her nape with the other. He looked into her eyes and, in one, long slow act, drove in all the way.

Her head went back and she gasped, at the same time as he summoned every ounce of will-power to stop the intense push from getting the best of him. He couldn't remember having experienced this kind of smouldering force before. It was like trying to catch and hold a fleet of flaming arrows in one hand.

He'd reined himself in and was moving again when the worst possible thing happened. Nuzzling up against his ear, she whispered his name.

A wave swept over his body at the same time as she trailed her fingertips up and down his sides. Goosebumps flashed over his skin and that fleet of arrows shot at his groin. He trembled, shuddered, tucked in his chin. But then she cupped his jaw and craned up to steal a tender yet urgent kiss. With her tongue edging lovingly over his, his erection throbbed and hardened to become near unmanageable.

Struggling to smile, he murmured against her mouth, "Did someone mention torture?"

Her laugh was more of a purr. "I can put you out of your misery."

Her velvet walls contracted around him, squeezing and holding while her teeth tugged his bottom lip. His hand dropped from the bedhead to iron up over her ribcage and knead her breast. As their movements blended and synchronised, he understood he'd never enjoyed an experience quite like this. The fire was so formidable that his blood had turned to lava.

It had nothing to do with their bond over her brother. Nothing to do with saving her life. It was physical, sure, but it was beyond that too. Every ion seemed to fuse in all the right places. She fitted him, he fitted her—everywhere.

Every way.

He took her mouth and kissed her hard as his skin steamed and pressure grew. A moment later she quietened beneath him, shrinking into herself and quivering while her breathing ceased altogether. With every tendon and muscle clenched, he withdrew fully, then filled her once more, hitting a place and a moment so high neither one would reach the ground again without jumping off.

Her fingers dug into his biceps as her frame arched high. The sky opened up—fierce, bright—and Gabriel dived into the light.

CHAPTER TEN

REMEMBERING the bliss of the previous passion-filled night, Nina eased into a satisfied smile a moment before blinking open her eyes to greet what she knew would be a fabulous new day.

With post-dawn shadows dancing over the quiet bedroom walls, and waves thundering on the shore, Nina rolled over. Awake only seconds, already her body ached for Gabriel's touch—and much more.

Her lover lay on his stomach, one muscled arm curled around his head, his bristled jaw resting upon the pillow. His thick sooty lashes were still and his highly kissable lips were parted. She listened to his deep breathing, which was almost a snore, as his broad bronzed back expanded and fell.

Her gaze filtered down.

The white sheet lay over his tight buns. The outline of his legs reached past the end of the bed. She remembered how that long, athletic body had pressed upon hers last night and a bright thrill sailed through her. No one made love the way he did. Physically he was supreme. As far as skill went, he was king. Even now his invisible line reeled her in. It had been there from the first, this unseen primal force that spoke to her soul. Chemistry? Yes.

And something more.

Nina watched him for long moments, enjoying that surreal feeling again. For the first time in so long she didn't feel the pressure to get up and "do." She could lie here all day with him if she wanted.

She no longer had a job to run off to.

Last night Gabriel had clobbered her with the news that he was, in fact, her childhood arch enemy number one: Gabe Turner. He'd followed that up by terminating her employ. Offering to set her up with a publishing job in Sydney didn't fix anything; she wouldn't go down that undeserving track again. But after he'd seduced her—after she'd surrendered and they'd made love half the night—neither had broached the subject of her termination again.

So where did she go from here?

A cool breeze blew up the gauzy curtains and Nina shivered. Rubbing her arms, she eased out from beneath the sheet. She tiptoed to the spare bedroom and entered its *en suite* bathroom. After a long shower, trying to figure out what the heck to do with her life from this point, she grabbed a plush robe off its hook and, fluff-drying her hair with a towel, emerged into the main room.

She stopped dead and caught her runaway breath.

Gabriel spun around to greet her while his dignified guest nodded cordially.

"I invited Dr Newman to check your ankle," Gabriel said.

"Mr Steele filled me in on your ordeal." The doctor indicated she should sit at the dinner table. "You're very lucky he came along when he did."

Nina tried to release the tension gripping her body, but what must the doctor think of her—an employee breaking that most sacred rule and spending the night with a guest? And, regardless of Gabriel saving her life, what right did he have calling the doctor without consulting her first? She felt like a child.

Clutching the robe closer to her neck, Nina cleared her throat. "Lucky…yes. But my ankle feels fine now, thank you."

The doctor pushed his bifocals to the bridge of his nose, then released the clip on his bag. "Nevertheless…"

Nina evaluated the situation. Clearly she was in no position to win a stand-off. Two against one, and her ankle was telling her to cop it on the chin and sit down.

Trying to look poised in her towelling robe, she crossed to a chair, and five minutes later the doctor's examination of her injuries was complete. He fished out some tablets, checked the label, and handed the pack over.

"Anti-inflammatories will help with that slight swelling and any pain." He snapped shut his bag and straightened his tie. "Keep the wounds clean, take it easy on your feet, and call me if you have any concerns."

Gabriel thanked the doctor for his time, and the moment the older man had let himself out Nina stood and gave Gabriel a look.

He arched his brows. "What?"

"I'm old enough to make my own appointments."

He gathered her near, stole three or four slow closed-mouth kisses from her lips, and the lines of her defence typically started to slide.

With a crooked grin, he rubbed the tip of his nose with hers. "I was only looking out for you."

His mouth lowered to kiss her again, but, feeling a little odd with Gabe Turner now that the daylight had come, she dodged and wove out of his arms. She knew he wasn't that proud, aloof teenager any more, but still…

She dug her hands into the robe's pockets. "Don't you think this is weird?"

"You mean how good we are together?"

"That we're together at all." She lowered herself into the couch. "I know time's supposed to heal all wounds, but you really didn't like me."

He tugged his ear. "I wouldn't say that."

She grinned. He might not *say* it, but she knew what he was thinking. Once upon a time he'd loathed the sight of her.

She sat back. "My parents never seemed to notice the battle going on between us, though. I remember one morning Dad said he thought Gabe Turner was a decent, hardworking boy. I chewed my cornflakes, scowling, and wished I never had to see you again."

As he folded down beside her, she stole a glance at him from beneath her lashes. Suddenly feeling like that fourteen-year-old again, she admitted, "My cheeks would burn whenever you walked by without so much as a hello. It was all I could do not to kick your shin."

He chuckled. "Why didn't you?"

"My mother said ladies never resort to violence." Her gaze shied away and her voice lowered. "So I tried to hurt you another way."

She'd let him know that while he might *think* he was hot stuff, he wasn't fit to wash her father's car.

She withered into herself and cringed. "I'm sorry, Gabe. I really was awful."

He was searching her eyes, checking to see if she was patronising him, but then his earnest face dissolved. "Ah, you weren't so bad."

He was being nice. She'd been horrid. But now, as an adult, she could acknowledge that annoying burning tension for what it had been…rumblings of sexual curiosity whenever Gabe Turner's impervious, marvellous presence entered a room. At fourteen, she'd been pretty clueless. Even if someone had pointed out that she'd had a crush on her brother's best friend, she doubted she'd have known what to do about it.

Had he felt attracted to her back then—even in a "she's a pain but still cute" kind of way? What would she have done if Geeky Gabe had silenced her snarky barbs with one perfect, penetrating kiss? At that age it wouldn't have been appropriate.

They'd grown up a lot since then.

She glanced over again, smiled, and swallowed a laugh. "You were such a dork."

"Hey, a lot of dorks have the smarts to make it in this world." He threaded his fingers behind his head. "Anthony, on the other hand, was a complete jock. We made an odd pair—" his gaze intensified "—but we understood each other."

She swung more towards him. "How did you two meet?"

A fond grin hitched up a corner of his mouth. "Anthony's bike had a flat, and I stopped on mine to help. The next day he offered to coach me at gym. I kicked butt with those grades that term, and our friendship went from there."

Remembering her carefree schooldays, Nina felt her heart contract. "I still miss him so much."

Gabriel's arms lowered and he took her hand. "After his accident I felt numb. It took me till midway through university, when I hooked up with Zane, before I got through a whole day without thinking about him."

"You liked uni?"

His thumb stroked the back of her hand. "My aunt worked two jobs to pay for my private school education. I owed it to her to do well." He grinned, remembering. "I wanted to buy her a penthouse in the heart of Sydney, and take her shopping at Tiffany's for genuine pearl earrings."

"*Very* nice." Her tone changed when she added, "Your aunt would be proud of you now."

"I have a way to go yet." He fixed her with a serious gaze. "But we're avoiding a very grave matter."

Nina landed back in the here and now.

Gabriel wasn't that adolescent geek any more. He was her boss, and he'd told her last night she was out of a job. She'd stayed with him last night, but was he about to break it to her that, nice as this little interlude had been, it was time to get her unemployed butt off his island? That their holiday fling was over?

"Thing is," he began, and his hand tightened around hers, "I want to know why you slipped out of bed this morning without at least one kiss to start my day."

She let go that breath. "A kiss?"

"At least one."

He closed in to take what he'd missed. At the same time the knocker fell on the front door. Nina reflexively pulled back, but he tugged her close again.

"Whoever it is," he murmured against her lips, "it's not important."

"How do you know?"

"Because nothing's as important as this."

His mouth covered hers, but the knocker sounded again, and again.

Growling, he pushed to his feet and held up an index finger. "Give me one minute."

But as he strode towards the door Nina gathered her whirling thoughts. This last day and a half she'd felt as if she were on a seesaw—one minute down and out, the next riding a rocket-ship-high.

Two things were certain. Gabriel needed to spend time on getting this island in shape. The working day had begun. It was time he got out there. Beyond that…as much as he inflated her tyres—as much as her switched-on body begged for his attention—she wouldn't set foot in that bedroom again until they'd sorted a few things out.

When Gabriel opened the door, his head pulled back. *Not* who he was expecting.

"April?"

What was his PA—make that *ex*-PA—doing here?

A tissue at her cheek, April dragged herself into the centre of the room. Her diminutive shoulders hunched and blonde hair came forward as she blew her nose.

"I'm not going through with it," she mumbled into the tissue.

Dumbfounded, Gabe followed her. "Through with…? You mean the wedding?"

She fixed him with accusing eyes. "I knew you wouldn't understand."

She'd spoken of nothing else for six months. She'd told him she couldn't live without this guy. She'd said how much her gown had cost, and he'd countered with, "That's outrageous!" Now she was in tears. Calling everything off. And people wondered why he wasn't rushing to tie any knots.

April's watery expression changed as her red-rimmed eyes focused on Nina. "Oh…sorry, I didn't realise you had company."

Nina was smiling uncertainly at their guest, while tugging the tie of her robe a little tighter. Gabriel exhaled. He guessed he should introduce them.

"April, this is Nina. Nina, this is April." He realised how this must look—as if he'd picked her up overnight—and while it shouldn't matter what April thought of anyone he saw, he added, "I've known Nina for years."

Preoccupied, April nodded, then spoke to herself more than to either of them.

"I've only known Liam twelve months. One short year." She collapsed into a chair and gazed unseeing at her sandalled pigeon-toed feet. "I felt as if we'd known each other for ever."

Nina's eyes questioned his. Gabriel shrugged, then edged forward. "What happened?"

"He wants me to sign a pre-nup."

"You didn't discuss it before now?"

In a daze, April shook her head. "He says his parents are insisting."

"I didn't think he had any money."

April slid him a dry look. "Compared to someone like you, no one has any money." She blew her nose again and spoke to Nina. "Would *you* sign a pre-nup?"

Nina blinked several times then stammered, "I—I don't think I'm the one to ask."

"You don't marry someone," April expounded, "commit your life and heart and soul, but have a conditional clause 'just in case.'"

Gabe stifled a groan. He couldn't see the problem. There were plenty of women out there ready to grab what they could. "Pre-nups are common practice these days."

"Well, these days suck!" April blew her nose again. "I'd love him no matter what."

He shrugged. "Then sign."

Nina spoke up. "If he trusted her, he wouldn't ask her to sign."

April sat a little straighter, then gave a solid nod.

Gabriel assessed the situation. He felt a lynching coming on, but realities couldn't be ignored. Pre-nups weren't heartless. They were useful tools in this modern-day, litigious, high-rate-of-divorce society. A better option was don't say I do. Don't move in together. Then property and other entitlement issues didn't become a problem.

Keep it simple.

Fun.

Brief.

His gaze skated to Nina before he crossed to the fridge, extracted juice, and very nearly grinned at a selfish thought. He looked across at April. "You can always come back and work for me."

She hadn't heard. "I can't see a way around this. Liam's gotten so testy all of a sudden. He even complained about the service here this morning."

Gabriel's business mind swooped in. "The service?" Nina's ears seemed to have pricked too.

April unfolded to her feet. "Don't worry. The service is great." Her brows pinched. "A little starchy, maybe." She rubbed her arms. "Too serious, or something. And that main restaurant could use a push into the twenty-first century—" She stopped and her shoulders came down. "But I'm not your PA any more." Her eyes began to fill. "I'm a woman who has to cancel her wedding."

A small sob escaped, and Gabriel strode over to give her a brotherly hug.

"It'll be okay. He's just got cold feet." He shivered, just thinking about it, and he was only a guest.

April blinked her big green eyes up at him. "You're sure that's all it is?"

"April, getting married is scary stuff."

When April's eyes flared and her bottom lip wobbled, Nina came forward.

"What Gabriel means is that it's a big step in any person's life." Nina sent him an "enough on the advice" look, and Gabriel sent back a "what did I say?" shrug. "I'm sure your fiancé will come around."

April heaved a sigh then dredged up a smile. "Thanks—" she acknowledged Gabriel "—both of you. I just hope you're right."

She dabbed her eyes a final time and Gabriel let her out.

At the door, he spun back and rubbed his hands. "Now, where were we?"

"We were feeling terrible for April," Nina reminded him as he spanned the distance separating them with "one-track mind" blinking like a neon sign on his forehead.

He threaded her fingers with his, drew two arcs in the air as he lifted her hands, and kissed each one while keeping his lidded gaze on hers. "If that's what they both want, they'll work it out."

"You're right. If he truly loves her, he'll see nothing should stand in their way."

Gabriel didn't object, but he didn't agree either. He merely began to lead her, hand in hand, towards his bedroom.

But she tugged back. "We need to talk."

"And we will." Hands on her waist, he bounced her up, like a human spear, into the air.

Caught between a laugh and a wail, she clutched onto his shoulders as he let her body slide, bit by bit, all the way down against his hard frame until her feet hovered an inch above the ground and their mouths finally met.

His kiss was drugging…so penetrating and involving that the sheer mastery of it—the undercurrent of ownership it conveyed—robbed her of any sense of time or place. Her nerve-endings were live wires by the time she realised he'd moved them into the bedroom… was lowering and tipping her back against the rumpled sheets and the jumble of downy pillows.

With deliberate calm, he set one fingertip to travel east over her collarbone. Her breasts warmed as his gaze followed the movement of his hand, which had skimmed nearer her cleavage. When his outside finger curved under her robe and over the mound of her left breast heat sizzled through her veins, condensing low in her belly before snaking down to stroke between her thighs.

Eyes drifting shut, she imagined him kneading her flesh, nipping and suckling those sensitive peaks again. When his breath brushed her cheek, her lips parted to take in more air. It was eight o'clock in the morning, and already she craved his mouth working over hers, his tongue delving, darting, showing no mercy and no signs of retreat.

His touch slid higher and found the curve of her jaw. The pad of his thumb circled under her chin before curling up over the rise and applying subtle pressure until her lips parted more. Her want simmered and steamed, a hot iron in the base of her belly. When she forced her eyes open his sparkling gaze was close, and she breathed out his name.

The hold on her jaw tightened as he brushed his bottom lip over hers, gently back and forth, up and then down. As if his erection was the South Pole, and her hips were super-charged magnets, she moved towards him, barely able to smother a moan of pure desire.

She was ready to give herself over to absolute passion when April's tear-stained face flickered into her mind's eye. Nina pushed the image aside—she would self-combust if she didn't feel him inside her again soon—but Gabriel's words…*getting married is scary stuff*…kept rolling over in her brain.

Scary was such an odd choice of word. It conjured up pictures of blood-sucking demons, or speeding around a hairpin turn with no brakes. Getting married *was* a serious affair—no argument. There was lots to consider. Precautions to take. But weddings shouldn't be *scary.*

She realised his mouth had lifted from her collarbone. He was peering into her eyes, concern creasing his brow.

"Nina, what's wrong? Your ankle hurting?"

She released the breath she hadn't known she'd been holding. "I can't stop thinking about April."

His nod was sombre. "It's a worry, but it's their business." His mouth nipped her chin. "Right now, I'm only concerned about you and me."

The warmth of his hand trailed up her leg, but a switch had been flicked on and Nina couldn't switch it back.

"You and me?" she repeated, then shimmied away and sat up. "You're right. We need to talk."

Two fingers trailed down her exposed thigh. "We can talk later."

She flipped the robe over her legs. "We should talk now."

His breath seemed to lock in his chest before he exhaled, rolled on one side and propped his weight on an elbow, head resting on his palm. "Okay. Shoot."

"This is where we are. We know each other's true identities, names, circumstances, past and present. I no longer have a job, and I don't want to be handed another one under the table. Finally, I'm being intimate with the man who gave me the axe."

He considered her summary, then nodded once. "That would be true and correct."

"So I'm thinking…" Her wry gaze darted left and right. "What happens now?"

"You heard the doctor. You need to stay off your feet. Since you're no longer entitled to staff quarters, I'm happy to offer you accommodation here until I leave on Monday."

She muttered, "Nothing like taking with one hand and giving with the other."

Was Gabriel friend or foe? Her guardian angel or the devil in disguise?

He exhaled patiently. "Fact is Gabriel Steele can't retain staff who don't measure up—but Gabe Turner can't turn Anthony's sister out on her ear." He covered her hand with his. "And the man who made love to you all night, who wants to make love to you now, can't either. I'll do anything to help you…except put you on another shift."

Nina chewed her lip. She wanted to tell him that if she was being sacked for impropriety she would argue he'd been the one to seduce *her.*

Sure, she'd been a willing participant. But if she'd spoken up sooner would her being a waitress have made any difference? They still would have slept together. She couldn't see that information stopping him at the crucial point.

"If you won't let me help you land a job," he added, "why not use your recuperation time here helping yourself? There must be connections of your own you haven't tried yet. Places you could contact." He squeezed her hand. "Sharpen up your résumé. Get on the phone."

She'd been ready to be difficult—from the moment he'd rescued her he'd always seemed so eager to run her life. But his idea held merit. And the simple truth was, despite the hot-and-cold journey they'd been on together, she wasn't ready to say goodbye to him yet.

And if she stayed here she might be able to convince him that she needed her job back. She wasn't a quitter. She had something to prove—to him, to the staff, and more so to herself. She hadn't earned her position here. She couldn't change that, but she could make up for it by working even harder and in some small way making a difference. If she was on a journey to rediscover herself, surely making that mistake right was part of it?

And, yes, in the meantime she could put her recovery time to good use—put her all into making sure that the next stop on her journey was the right one, however hard that was going to be. She took a deep breath, praying Gabe would accept what she knew she had to say next.

"Okay," she agreed. "You have a deal." He beamed as he craned up to cement the deal with a kiss, but Nina's hand appeared between their mouths. "On one condition."

He curled away. "I don't like conditions."

"Our relationship will be platonic from here on in."

"Are you *mad?* I can't agree to that."

"I'll give you one very good reason why you should."

He arched a brow. "I'll give you a better one why I shouldn't."

When he came nearer she slipped further away.

"You're on this island to implement the changes needed to turn this place around. You have a finite amount of time, till next Monday, to put to maximum use." She cocked her head. "Tell me truthfully. Wouldn't you rather lie in bed all day with me than go out and strategise with Mr Dorset and co?"

His eyes narrowed. "Clearly that's a trick question. We're living in paradise. We're great together." His eyes sparkled over his grin. "Why not enjoy it while it lasts?"

"I'll tell you why. It's after eight now. Your working day should have already begun. You should be out there knuckling down, making sure you do what you've come here to do. Turn this place around. Make changes for the better."

As she planned to do.

"The problems will still be there at nine." He moved in to kiss her, but she pushed him away as best she could.

"While we're in an intimate relationship you'll be distracted. Then you're going to be upset for letting yourself be sidetracked from your work." Committed to the idea, she shrugged. "For your own good, I'm taking that temptation away."

He shifted her robe and feather-kissed her shoulder. "Did I mention I can multi-task?"

She tugged her robe back. This was a gorgeous place, and he was an amazing lover, but… "If you want me to stay here—if you really want to help me—then you're going to have to let me help you too. I won't loll around with you in bed half the day and then watch you explode like you did at the cabin yesterday because you're angry with yourself for slacking off."

"Being here is different—"

"Yes, it's worse. By tomorrow everyone will know I'm shacked up with a guest."

And she'd thought she'd been a target before. It would be worse for her when it was discovered that Gabriel Steele—the guest she'd temporarily moved in with—was everyone's new boss.

She might as well ask.

"When are you going to tell the staff who you are?"

"Not this visit," he stated. "There's enough to look at with the managers and facilities."

"Don't you want to give them a chance to speak out on what *they* think could make a difference? They're the ones who keep this place ticking over."

The bungalow telephone extension pealed and, closing his eyes, Gabriel rested one stacked fist on his brow. "You're going to tell me to get that, aren't you?"

You bet. "No rest for the wicked."

He sprang over, about to decimate her with a take-no-prisoners kiss, but then a shadow chased over his face and he backed away.

"I hate to admit it, but you're right. As much as I want to stay here with you, I have to do what I have to do."

As he left her alone in his bedroom, Nina let out a long breath. There was another reason she'd put forward her ultimatum, and it was as significant as Gabriel's need to focus on his work, rather than on sex. Self-preservation.

They'd been together perhaps thirty-six hours and, remarkable as it might sound, she'd never felt more deeply about any man. Convincing herself she could have more with Gabriel than a holiday fling would be easier than demolishing a piece of Chef Reynolds' chocolate marshmallow tart. She felt so right when they were together—so perfectly, wonderfully right—as though, even if she never belonged anywhere else, it was okay because she *did* belong in his arms.

But she'd known before that his interest in her was casual, and after his admission about getting married being scary she'd be a fool to think he was after anything remotely long-term. At the moment her self-worth was shaky enough. The last thing she needed was to fall in love with someone who couldn't love her back.

CHAPTER ELEVEN

Late Friday morning, Gabriel returned after his third meeting with the Diamond Shores managers.

He stepped into the bungalow's foyer, wringing his tie loose and expecting Nina to come bounding out, like she usually did, to hear any news. He'd taken her advice and introduced himself to the staff. Since Wednesday he'd met with the resort conference people, recreation personnel, wait staff and, at nine this morning, housekeeping.

The exercise had gone well.

He jogged down the two timber steps that linked the foyer to main room and threw a look around the gleaming furniture and potted palms. Dropping his tie over the back of a bar stool, he moved onto the balcony.

The sky was a flawless early-summer blue, the air was fresh with the scent of brine, and in his private pool, stretched out before the beach, Nina was doing laps. Gabriel's testosterone levels swirled to the roof. He was a heartbeat away from kicking off his shoes, shucking off his clothes and diving straight in.

Nina in a bikini was impossible to pass up.

The other morning she'd told him that she wanted to downgrade their relationship to platonic. She didn't

want to be a distraction when he had so much to accom-
plish here. She'd been right. He *would* rather fool
around with her than knuckle down to the massive task
of returning profitability to this establishment. And so
he'd kept his distance—no easy feat.

But at no time had he actually agreed to her terms.

During business hours things were moving in the
right direction, but when night fell the tension back at
the bungalow was tripwire-tight. Lounging in the living
room, or out on the deck, sometimes Gabriel had to bite
his inside cheek to stop from swooping over and
stashing Nina away in his room. Watching her concentrate on doing a crossword, or chewing her nails over
some reality TV show, was akin to passing out in the
world's hottest sauna when the most delectable,
quenching nectar was waiting an arm's length away.

He wasn't alone in feeling that fire. He'd caught
Nina's hidden looks when he passed, noticed the way
her breathing deepened whenever they were close.

Now, with her wet, pumped and half-naked in that
pool, was the time to revisit that ultimatum of hers.
They were leaving the island on Monday. If she felt half
as sexually frustrated as he did, she couldn't refuse the
idea of one last hold-onto-your-seatbelts romp.

Moving to the edge of the pool, he hunkered down
onto the terracotta tiles. He watched her graceful form
glide through the water before she came up for air a foot
away. She pushed hair from her face, drove down a big
breath, then coughed it back up when she saw him.

He chuckled at her surprise and eventual smile
before holding out his hand. "I've given myself the rest
of the day off."

"Welcome home."

She took his hand, he helped her out, and she

grabbed a towel off a nearby lounger. He hid his disappointment when that delicious red bikini was part-way concealed as she wiped down her hair and tanned arms.

"I heard you were speaking with Tori today," she said.

His gaze skated up from what he could see of her legs.

"News travels fast." He rubbed the back of his neck. "Remind me who Tori is again."

"Tall, blonde. She might've been wearing watermelon wedge earrings."

"Ah, yes. She had quite a bit to say."

"Anything useful?"

"The gist was the same as my previous staff meetings. She'd like to see protocol and activities relaxed. Less formal. More fun. Or at least room for that somewhere on the island."

"Maybe you should wear Bermuda shorts to the next meeting."

He mock frowned. "I'll take that under advisement. I've been looking through stacks of guest comments," he went on, moving to the sun loungers. "A lot mentioned updating too."

"Facilities?"

"Policies, entertainment, staff uniforms."

"Tori and her earrings will be pleased to hear it."

"I have plenty to go on."

Lashing the towel under her arms, sarong-style, she crossed over.

"What about a staff buddy system? If the longer-serving staff members had younger ones under their care and tutelage we'd get a better vibe through the ranks. There's nothing worse than being told to fold the napkins a certain way and having no idea but being too frightened to ask." Her expression wavered. "I suppose I should have known…"

"No, no. Point taken. Everyone needs to get more involved with the next guy—or gal."

"If guests saw a real camaraderie among the staff, I bet they'd relax more too. You could start a new ad campaign, promoting a more laid-back slant."

Interested, he made a mental note.

"I have some other news." He sat on the end of the nearest lounger. "April's wedding is back on. Her fiancé stood up to his parents' demands and is marrying April with or without the pre-nup."

Nina punched the air—*yes!*—then sat down too. "Good for him!"

"I want you to come with me."

Her animated face froze. "To the wedding?"

"I've put in a special request that the desserts must be doubly to die for."

He could imagine the cogs spinning in her mind. *Should she? Shouldn't she?* Did partnering him at a wedding breach the platonic line she'd drawn in the sand? Mere semantics. That snag would be fixed soon enough anyway.

Finally her expression eased and she nodded. "Sure. I'd love to go."

"Done." He stood and pulled her up too. "Now, grab some shorts and a top. We need a change of scenery."

By noon they were aboard a thirty-six-foot sailing yacht, heading out for a leisurely cruise around some of the other Great Barrier Reef islands. After they'd left the bay and were in open waters, Gabriel let Nina steer.

Her hands clutched the wheel so tightly her knuckles turned white. But he was standing close by, enjoying the view of salt air whipping through her hair while seafaring exhilaration built on her face. When they anchored near a coral ledge, they stripped to swimsuits and slipped into the crystal-clear water. With masks and snorkels they floated out together and wove over a world of marine life that darted between fingers of jade, pink, aqua and vermilion coral.

Iridescent blue angel fish, gold and white striped harlequin tuskfish, parrot fish, butterfly fish…so vivid and brilliant and clear. He chuckled to himself at the fresh wide-eyed wonder behind her mask when she pointed out an ancient turtle swimming by, close enough to touch.

After they'd climbed back on board and showered off, taking advantage of the dwindling breeze, Gabriel manoeuvred the yacht into a remote island cove. There was barely a breath of wind left by the time he dropped anchor.

Perfect. The weather report had been spot-on.

He laid out a picnic blanket on the timber deck beneath the shade of the sail, while Nina organised prawns, oysters, pineapple and fresh mango for a late lunch spread. He poured Chardonnay into plastic goblets and she peeled two enormous prawns. Looking up at the mast, then at the palm trees fringing the unpopulated island's white-lined shore, she bit into the flesh. Chewing, and still looking around, she wiped her fingers on a paper towel.

"Everything's so quiet," she said.

"No wind."

Stretching out her legs and resting back on one arm, she accepted a goblet of wine. "Don't sails need wind? How do we get back?"

"I have oars." He raised his glass. "Cheers."

She smiled. "I'm getting an interesting visual. But really…"

While she sipped, he peered up at the vigilant gulls wheeling overhead. Not a cloud in the sky. Plenty of food and good wine. A beautiful, sassy woman, in an amazing flaming red bikini—who wanted to leave?

He shrugged. "We'll have to wait it out." No need for her to know about the inboard motor.

She sat up. "How long do you think?"

"You have something to rush back to?"

"Not a thing."

He wasn't quite sure how to take her tone. Had she done all she could with regard to finding another job—sending out more résumés, contacting industry friends— Or had she resigned herself to packing up and leaving in a couple of days without a job to go to?

She reached for one side of a mango and turned the skin inside out. Juice exploded and streamed down her forearms. Rushing to suck the fruit, she tried to capture what she could, and a fierce coil of awareness lassoed and tugged at his groin. He drove down a breath and blew it quietly out. She was sexy without trying—but was she doing that on purpose?

She continued to suck and lick the soft orange flesh and then, as if she hadn't known how captivating her ingesting fruit could be, she threw a glance across and smiled.

"I'll be sticky after this," she said. "We could go for another swim."

Or we could make love.

She inclined her head. "Did you say something?"

"I said I don't want another swim."

When he downed half his wine, she blinked twice and her cheeks pinked up beneath her wide-brimmed hat. It was becoming harder to hide his autonomic responses. Harder to pretend he wanted to. His jaw was tight, his stomach too. The back of his neck felt on fire.

"You must be starved," she said.

A tiny rapid pulse beat at the side of her throat. He felt the same rhythm hammering away in his blood.

"Here." She handed over a delicacy. "These oysters look delicious."

Keeping his gaze on hers, he lifted a shell and slid the oyster into his mouth. The salty, slippery, exotic taste only teased him more. It was all he could do to keep his gaze from wandering to her cleavage…to her thighs.

Her bikini wasn't *naughty,* exactly; the fabric covered all the necessary bits. But the legs were cut intriguingly high and her womanly hips were so curvy. Her breasts were pulled up and looked so full that the temptation to drag her over was one he could barely contain.

No doubt reading his mind and wanting to cool it, she turned a little away, curled her legs beneath her and selected another oyster. But as her fork lifted the oyster from its shell Gabriel noticed her breathing had changed. Deeper. Quicker. And the blush which had started on her cheeks had radiated down the slim column of her throat. As the burn at his nape flashed like wild fire over the rest of his body, he clenched his hand against the urge to lean over and press his lips to her throat and that heat.

She edged a plate towards him. "Have some mango. They're so juicy."

He groaned. "I noticed."

"We had two huge mango trees in our backyard. Do you remember?"

If she wanted to change the subject that they weren't discussing, it wouldn't work.

"Trees?" He set down his goblet. "I don't recall."

"Sure you do. You and Anthony stuffed yourselves so much that summer Mum thought you'd throw up."

Gabriel's mind flashed back and he had to grin. He remembered Anthony's mouth stained orange, skins all over the backyard. They'd been barely able to move they'd eaten so much.

Gabriel cleared his throat and moved closer to Nina. He didn't want to discuss old times now.

She bit into a slice of pineapple and chewed contemplatively. "You never stayed at our house for dinner. You always went home to eat."

"Faith liked having family meals around the table," he summed up, then held up the bottle. "More wine?"

Nina declined, then dropped her gaze. "Gabe, you don't have to tell me if you don't want to, but...I was wondering what happened to your mother? Who was she before she had you?"

He lowered the bottle. As mood-killers went, that was a ten. He hadn't spoken about that with anyone. But if Nina wanted to know they'd be here for a while. He guessed he *could* share.

"You want the unabridged version?"

"If you want."

He drove his fingers through his hair and held them there while he thought back.

"Faith and my mother Darlene's parents worked on their landlord's dairy farm. The girls had a good mother and father, but the only speck of luxury in their lives came when they went to the cinema. Darlene worshipped Hollywood films and dreamed of marrying the next Robert Redford or Paul Newman. She planned to live in Los Angeles, but fell pregnant before she'd saved enough for a fare. She didn't tell my father. At eighteen, she didn't want to give her baby up, but she didn't want to wind up with a going-nowhere-nobody either. She had her heart set on a famous, dashing, wealthy husband."

Nina spoke gently. "She didn't think your father was good enough?"

"He couldn't give her the fantasy life she wanted. So Darlene shifted in with Faith, who'd moved to the city. Darlene had her baby, then set out to find a real man." He cocked his head. "My words, not hers, but you get my drift."

Nina got his drift, all right. His mother had robbed Gabriel of the chance to get to know his dad and vice versa. On top of that she'd left him with an echo that reached from past to present, from father to son...

Not a real man.

Nina's verbal darts all those years ago, insinuating he didn't measure up, wouldn't have helped. She'd been young and foolish. After that story she could only imagine how deeply her taunts must have cut.

"That search took my mother to all kinds of interesting places—including bars." A muscle in his jaw flexed twice. "One night she didn't come home. The police said she'd just run out on her responsibilities. I was four. When I was eight they charged a man with the rape and murder of three women in the district over the preceding four years."

Her breath caught.

So his mother *hadn't* abandoned her little son. Cold comfort, though, given the circumstances.

His palm lay on the deck. She covered it lightly with her own. "And your father found you years later?"

"I found him." His hand flipped over to hold hers. "Gary Steele remained a bachelor and became extremely successful in advertising. Quite an irony as far as my mother's ambitions were concerned."

Nina shifted uneasily. Gabriel was almost gloating that his father had avoided what could have been a messy relationship with Darlene. But his mother had disappeared from her son's life by the time Gabriel was four. Hadn't he ever wondered about his father during that time?

"Why didn't your aunt try to find your dad?"

"She sent a letter a while after my mother vanished but never got a reply. Gary said he'd moved from that address years before to live in the UK briefly and never received it. Faith believed, right or wrong, that she'd best leave good enough alone. I didn't blame her. Not at all. She sacrificed a lot to make sure I had what I needed."

"Is that why you're so focused on success now?"

His chin tipped up. "Hmm?"

"To prove to the ghost of your mother," she murmured, "that you're a *real man?*"

He gave her a wily look. "Big leap."

"Not really. My father was the same. He worked like a dog to prove himself to *his* father."

Her grandfather had been a tyrant, with beady eyes, a bushy beard and not a kind word for anyone other than his financial advisor and his bridge partner. Whenever the family had frequented his mausoleum of a house she and Jill had stayed glued to her father's side. Anthony had said Grandad was Blackbeard come back to life, only meaner.

"My dad built on an already successful engineering empire," she went on, "then spent every moment worried about holding it together."

His thumb rubbed the back of her hand and his head angled. "What happened to the money?"

"After my father passed away my mother went through the lot like tap water."

"Hate to speak ill of your mother, but I bet your dad's rolling over in his grave."

"Meredith always had a champagne taste. My father loved her extravagant nature and bought her way too much. Jewellery, cars, holidays at the best resorts around the world. She got used to over-the-top. Difference was, when my father was alive he'd been able to step on the brakes when need be."

"Poor guy. Worked his entire life for nothing."

"If he hadn't worked so hard maybe he'd still be around. Stress is a killer."

His pale eyes darkened as he leaned closer. "I vote no stress today."

Nina's skin flashed hot. The intent in his voice, in his eyes, said only one thing. He wanted to kiss her. Way more than kiss.

But, no matter how the air snapped and crackled whenever they were together, she'd made herself clear the other day. Sex was best kept out of the equation. Firstly, she was a distraction he didn't need right now. Secondly, unfairly or not, he'd dismissed her from her job. Thirdly, if she got any more involved—if she fell any deeper—he'd most likely take her heart too.

She shucked back her shoulders. "I won't play this game. I know what you're thinking."

"Tell me."

He tipped nearer still and, heart beating fast, she tipped back. "I thought we'd put this behind us."

His eyes smouldered. "Guess you thought wrong."

As his gaze flicked over her lush parted lips, he slid a hand around her nape to bring her close. But she pulled back, and the first inkling of suspicion faded up in her eyes. She blinked rapidly, as if her mind was catching up with the evidence at hand.

"You planned this, somehow, didn't you?" She snapped a glance at the sky, the sail. "I mean mooring here, when the breeze was set to run out."

He pressed a sensual kiss to her bare shoulder. "Now, how could I do that?"

"You *knew* I wouldn't be able to escape."

"Do you want to escape?"

She growled in her throat, but this time didn't pull away. "You're twisting things."

He wound her arm around his neck.

"Organising this boat," she said. "Sailing out here… All the time you were planning, saving this up—"

His mouth caressed the sensitive spot below her collarbone. "And I'm about to blow."

She stiffened against him. A tense moment passed before the pressure building between them seemed to ignite, expand and then release. After letting out a long-suffering sigh, she trembled and finally furled her fingers up the back of his hair.

Sighing softly, she grazed her cheek against his. "Oh, Gabe, I'm about to blow too."

He smiled to himself.

Score one for the weather man.

He lovingly nipped her chin. "What happened to putting this behind us?"

"What happened to no escape?"

He was about to kiss her the way he'd dreamed of kissing her these past drought-ridden days when something—or someone—seemed to tap him on the shoulder. When he tried to ignore it, the tap came again.

He swore to himself. What a time to get the guilts.

He held her arm and asked, in all earnestness, "Nina,

I want to know if you have any real concerns about this…"

Her lips feathered over his. "I'll let a real man kiss them away.'

When she pulled him down on top of her, he happily fell.

"Lord above, I've missed this," he murmured, snatching kiss after kiss while her sexual hunger spiked and relapsed into that raw, lethal need. "I missed you so much."

She ground herself up against him while her fingers dug into his biceps, and all thought but for him dropped away.

Drunk with passion, they rolled over on the blanket, one way then the other, their mouths locked as their hands sought out places that ached for attention. Her breasts burned to know the stiff, moist stroke of his tongue. Her sex throbbed to feel him deep inside her. When he ripped her bikini top off, the thrust of her desire for him hit like a nuclear blast.

His mouth on her throat, he dragged off her bikini bottoms. She yanked at his fitting trunks while her other hand fanned the warm rock of his chest. When more of his scent filled her lungs she felt almost too dizzy with longing to breathe.

He found her wet and hypersensitive. With one mighty arcing action he swept the plates of food well aside and then kissed her again, his tongue edging over hers, probing deeper, as if no matter how long or how hard they stayed connected he could never get enough.

She held him close, one knee measuring his side before his mouth left hers and his head lowered. When his lips suctioned around her nipple, drawing her deeply into his mouth, bright fountains of colour were released in her head. Her fingers knotted in his hair and that leg coiled over his back.

As the fever took hold, and her arousal clamoured at the ceiling, she reached, trying to tug again at his trunks. He wrangled out of his wet shorts. A second later his pulsing erection pushed against her hip, then cooler air brushed her body as his heat drew away.

Dizzy with need, she opened her eyes. Craning up onto her elbows, she was ready to cry out—*Don't you dare leave me now.*

But he was kneeling over her, his fists coming down either side of her shoulders. His eyes were stormy and his nostrils flared with the effort to take in enough air. Then he slowly lowered, to tease her, rubbing the head of his erection over her intimate folds, making her bloom and throb all the more. When she moved provocatively beneath him, teasing him back, his control snapped in two. He entered her more roughly than he'd intended, hitting a place that made her jump and rock her head to one side.

Concerned, he grabbed her shoulder. "Nina, are you all right?"

She wet her lips and sighed long and loud. "Do it again."

A hot, lazy smile curved his lips before he filled her once more, and a jet of high-octane sparks showered up, setting every part of her alight. Nina was washed away on the climbing tide. The energy spiralled higher, condensed tighter, until the heart of her cried out for release. But another part of her wanted this ecstasy to last—wanted this fire to rage on and on and out of control.

When he sank into her again, the force of her orgasm

ripped a cry from her lips. Pulsating energy contracted, then tore her apart, spraying sparks of pleasure through her blood. She was vaguely aware of his release too, of his fingers digging into her hip, of his chest rubbing high against hers as he shuddered and let his heat flow.

Curling her arms up over her head, Nina pressed against her lover's hard, slick body, soaking up the peak of their magic. And exhausted moments later, when he lay beside her and pulled a corner of the blanket over them both, she knew she'd never felt more content.

She was never more herself than when Gabriel held her like this.

He was the perfect rogue. A fantastic lover. But anyone could fathom why he wasn't after long-term. Why marriage was *scary*.

Scars from his past. No belief in happily-ever-afters. He'd lived his whole life knowing his mother had put her ambition before her little son's best interests. He'd deserved to know his father. He'd deserved a mother who hadn't roamed around searching for her fantasy meal-ticket at night. No wonder he was cynical.

But Nina hoped he would discover real love one day. She could imagine him standing at the altar, wearing a crisp black suit, his tanned hands clasped before him, his smile serene. She could see the love in his eyes, the boundless commitment on his face and wished…a silly romantic's wish.

Nina wished the bride was her.

CHAPTER TWELVE

Nina enlisted the help of Julie LaFoy, the manager of the island's many well-stocked boutiques, to help her with a dress for April's wedding.

The gown she chose had been drastically discounted—at least that was what an excited Julie had said. The style blended "red carpet" with chic sarong. Coupled with a pair of elegant matching heels, Nina felt like an island princess. But no one outshone April on her big day.

April wore a traditional gown of white satin, with a sweeping fairytale veil. When she walked down the outdoor aisle, the groom's face split into an adoring smile and one hundred guests audibly sighed. The ceremony was brief, but heartfelt, and when the bride threw her bouquet it sailed right towards Nina's head. She ducked, and the woman behind her squealed on snaring the prize.

As the music went into party mode, and canapés were served, Gabriel took Nina's hand and led her to the dance floor, which was set up beneath an open marquee. When Nina spotted Mr Dorset hovering around the fringes, making sure everything was in order, a shudder shot up her spine. But when Gabriel gathered her in his arms and held her eyes with his she forgot everything other than how her heart wouldn't stop thumping. How much she loved being his date.

This time last week she would never have dreamed she'd be dancing with the most attractive man in Australia… Well, he was to her. His scent, his feel, the way his eyes spoke only to her… This might have been *their* wedding day. She might even believe that the intense depth of his look meant he was thinking the same.

If wishes came true…

With other couples joining them on the floor, Gabriel dance-stepped her smoothly around.

"Your gown is something else," he said, in a low, appreciative voice.

A rush of pride made her glow. The gown was of softest tangerine silk, cinched high on the side of the waist with a diamanté clasp before falling in weightless folds to her ankles. "Feminine," Julie had said. "Timeless…"

His hot fingertips skimmed up and down her back. "I like the colour. The cut. It looks exquisite on you."

The warmth of her blush deepened. He'd told her three times already.

They'd danced for several moments, moving as one to the music, before he murmured near her ear, "I haven't held you for hours."

"Two, to be exact."

"Two hours too long." He grazed a seductive kiss over her brow and she quivered when his lips veered south.

She would never tire of his compliments. Not that this affair would last. In fact, as much as she loathed to admit it, the sooner "they" ended, the better. The

way he looked at her—with a heart-pumping combination of protectiveness and desire—she was in
danger of convincing herself she meant way more to
him than she did. That kind of self-delusion could
only pave a fast track to emotional suicide. She would
not fall in love with someone who couldn't commit
and love her back.

She needed to accept this relationship for what it was:
an abstract version of a holiday fling. Gabriel saw it that
way. In his mind, he had his life and she had hers—or
would again when she got off this island. When that
would be depended on how he answered her question.

She wanted a chance to somehow validate her place
here, in the staff's eyes as well as in her own. She
wanted her position here back. If she did a good enough
job, surely Gabriel would be proud of her too.

Her cheek was resting on his lapel when an almighty
crash exploded directly behind them. Heart in her
throat, Nina spun around. A young waitress stood by
the nearby cake table, hands over her mouth, her eyes
wide with shock. At the waitress's feet lay a stack of
broken plates. The top tier of the multi-layered wedding
cake was splattered over the debris. Nina shuddered.
She could just see Mr Dorset's outraged face now.

She rushed over to help, automatically picking up
broken crockery. She caught the stunned girl's eye.

"Run and get a dustpan," she said. "A bin and some
paper towels."

Nina hadn't seen the girl before. Around eighteen,
she must be new. She reminded Nina of herself her first
week here. Uncertain. Wanting to do well. Failing
before she'd been given half a chance. No doubt this
woman had experience, but accidents happened, and
Nina wasn't prepared to stand back and let her get

bawled out without standing beside her. She knew too well what it felt like to cop it alone.

The waitress rushed off at the same time as Gabriel knelt down. "Nina, you're a guest here tonight." His hand held hers. "Leave that. Cake's getting on your gown."

"It'll be cleaned up twice as fast if I help."

"There's plenty of staff—"

She cut him off with a look. "I can't stand back and watch."

The waitress returned, and she and Nina dropped broken crockery into the mini-bin. Nina caught the waitress's expression: her blue eyes were wet with gratitude. Nina smiled back and they picked up the pace.

April appeared, hands clasped beneath her crestfallen face. "My cake!"

Mr Dorset was behind her, his expression pinched. Knowing this was Gabriel Steele's affair, he would be doubly ready to vent his wrath.

A puffed-up Dorset had opened his mouth, ready to come down on the young waitress, but something fierce inside Nina leapt, and she stepped up to stand between them.

"I'm sorry, Mr Dorset," she said, feeling braver and more vulnerable than she had in her life. "I knocked the table corner when I passed. I'll pay for any damage."

While Mr Dorset eyed her with obvious suspicion, Gabriel stepped forward too. "Everything's fine here, Dorset. Thanks for your concern."

And as he said the words three wait staff bee-lined it over... Maureen, Judy, and usually grave-faced Jim Olsen too.

"We'll take care of this," Maureen told Nina as she

lowered herself down beside the younger waitress, and Jim produced a dust pan and brush from thin air.

Gabriel held April's shoulders. "There's plenty of cake left." His voice was quiet. "I'll make it up to you, hon—I promise."

April looked between them both, then her brows opened up before she sighed on a forgiving smile. "The day has been so perfect. Something little had to go wrong."

But Nina was too choked up to respond. Before she'd begun work here she wouldn't have dreamed of intervening in a scene like this the way she had. But, no matter the consequences, she'd felt compelled to protect that young waitress in a way no one had stepped up to protect her. And yet Maureen, Judy, Jim…they knew what she'd done, and by their actions they were saying they approved. Tonight, in her finery, she should have felt more alienated than ever from the staff, yet for the first time since arriving on this island she didn't feel like an outsider.

Mr Dorset answered April. "The bride's only job today is to look beautiful. We'll take care of this."

Before Mr Dorset moved off, his gaze found Nina's. Imagination, perhaps, but she thought she recognised a thin glimmer of respect in his eyes.

After Nina had freshened up, she and Gabriel danced for several more songs. Later they chatted with the other guests, and shared a piece of delicious vanilla wedding cake. When numbers began to dwindle they said goodbye and good luck to the bride and groom, and headed off.

Nina was floating. Aside from that unfortunate accident with the plates and the cake, it had been a wonderful day—for so many reasons. Firstly because tonight had been the first time she'd felt in any way accepted by other members of the staff. She'd never forget their expressions and willingness to help after she'd stood up to Dorset. She believed more than ever that the staff buddy system she'd recommended to Gabriel had real merit.

Just as importantly, the evening had been wonderful because of the way Gabriel had genuinely enjoyed himself—despite his aversion to weddings. She'd almost wanted to point it out—*See. It wasn't so scary after all.*

But now her adrenaline had been spent, and she was ready to retire to the bungalow, to be alone with Gabriel and soak up what remained of their time together. Only one more day…

But once they were out of the private party area he headed in the opposite direction, away from the bungalow.

Nina glanced over her shoulder. In the far distance she could make out the hazy lights from his deck, the extra-tall palm trees that marked his front door.

"Where are we going?"

He shrugged out of his dinner jacket and draped it across her shoulders. His subtle masculine scent wrapped around her. "You'll see."

They climbed a winding path, leaving the resort's lights and sounds behind. As the shadows grew darker, and the rustle of fronds grew louder, the track sloped up and became littered with fragrant petals. Then fairy-lights appeared on either side of the track, twinkling so brightly they seemed eager to lead them to some secret, hidden place.

What was at the end of the track?

His arm was around her waist. She leaned towards his solid heat. "This is very mysterious."

He held up his free hand and crossed two fingers. "Mystery and I are like that."

At the top of the modest incline Nina stopped and held her throat as her breath hitched and heart flipped over. A cashmere-soft-looking blanket was laid out before a cosy fire that licked orange and blue flames around a fat crackling log. A silver bucket, holding a bottle of champagne, sat backstage. The scene was circled by those same sweet-smelling blooms, a sea of petals surrounding their own private island.

A rush of tears prickled the backs of her eyes. It was simple, inviting, and possibly the most romantic thing a man had ever done for a woman.

Her knees suddenly watery, she held his arm tighter. "Gabe, this is…amazing."

He helped her down onto the blanket, then moved to the ice bucket. While she dashed away a happy tear, he poured two glasses as an ocean of stars watched over them from their black velvet sky.

His dinner shirt a beacon against the shadows, he handed over a glass and lowered himself beside her.

"It was such a lovely day," she sighed.

"I've been to a lot of weddings but, yes, this one was special."

"Because it was April's?"

"Because you were there." While her heartbeat skipped he sipped, then set his glass aside. "I liked that they wrote their own vows."

"Lots of couples do."

He peered off into the distance and smiled absently. "I liked what Liam said about marrying her being his greatest achievement."

She smiled, remembering too. "I think they'll be very happy."

They watched the lights twinkle for several moments, content to sip champagne and listen to the night birds' calls.

"Thanks for not blowing the whistle on me when I helped that poor waitress tonight," Nina finally said. She'd wanted to say it all night, but now seemed appropriate, away from prying eyes and ears.

"I felt sorry for her, poor kid."

"Mr Dorset wouldn't have."

His chin came up. "To be fair, he has a responsibility to keep the level of service high."

"And the best way to do that is by putting the fear of God into the staff?"

He drew her near and she, a little stiffly, rested her cheek on his broad shoulder again. He didn't want to discuss business tonight. Neither did she. She'd much rather drink in the lake of lights flickering below and enjoy the quiet. Enjoy this time alone.

Maybe if things had been different, if they'd met again under different circumstances, where she'd felt more herself...

But she was forgetting. While she might be trying to overcome and make sense of some personal hurdles at the moment, Gabriel was comfortable with who he was, what he wanted, which was to enjoy this "fling in paradise" while it lasted. As much as she might want to dream, her destiny didn't lie with him.

When some time later he poured the last of the wine, she took the empty bottle to examine it.

"If we put a message in this bottle and threw it out to sea, I wonder where it would end up? I wonder who would read it?"

"What would your message say?" he asked, but before she could answer, he piped up, "I know. We could date it, include a phone number, and tell the recipient to ring and pass on the relevant details."

She laughed. "That's the most logical, geekish thing I've ever heard."

He gave in to a smile. "If I ever need to send a message, I promise to give it more thought."

She set the bottle down. "Gabriel, can I ask you to give something else some more thought?"

"Anything."

"I'd like my job back."

His brows knitted. "We've discussed that."

"You're not still angry with me for not finding the right moment to tell you about my situation here, are you?"

"Of course not."

"I can't pretend I want to be a waitress the rest of my life," she went on. "Simple truth is I needed the money to make ends meet. I was desperate when my friend gave me the heads-up, but from the moment I landed I wondered if I'd made a huge mistake. I made myself ill wondering if, rather than helping, accepting that job had thrown me further off course." She rested her hand on his. "I don't expect you to understand— it's so hard to explain—but I need to finish this, Gabe. Particularly after tonight. I need to find out who I am at the end of this road before I can travel down the next."

He searched her eyes for a long moment, then exhaled and nodded deeply. "If that's what you truly want…if that's what you need…consider yourself reinstated."

She sat straighter. She'd convinced him? "You mean it?"

He smiled. "I'll call Dorset tomorrow. See how soon you can get back on the roster."

She flung her arms around him and squeezed. She'd never dreamed being a waitress again would make her so happy.

"This means so much—and I promise," she said, drawing back and crossing her heart, "I won't let you down."

CHAPTER THIRTEEN

LATE the next morning, Gabriel strode into Ziggies, Diamond Shore's most popular café by the beach. The ocean air was fresh and salty, but with a hint of coconut oil wafting in from the nearest pool. Riots of colourful flowers glistened with beads from the automatic sprinklers' earlier run. He was alone, bleary-eyed and testy. He needed his second cup of coffee.

But his irritation had less to do with caffeine deprivation and more to do with the phone call he'd made earlier that morning. Last night Nina had asked for her job back. She'd spoken about mistakes and roads travelled, and she'd seemed so anguished and sincere by the end of it he couldn't refuse. If it was that important to her, he would make it happen.

Dorset's response on the phone this morning hadn't been what Gabriel had expected. The older man had jumped in and announced that Nina could go back to work right away. Gabriel suspected Nina's actions in helping that waitress at the wedding might have had something to do with Dorset's change of heart. He, too, had approved of Nina's courage and willingness to pitch in, even while wearing an evening gown. She certainly wasn't the Nina that Gabe Turner had once known. She wasn't even the woman he'd met a week ago. Every day she seemed to grow.

Now, as he strode into the café grounds, his mind wound back to the previous night, when they'd returned to the bungalow after the wedding. He'd peeled that delicious dress from her shoulders and taken her to his bed. Their every touch had seemed heightened. The scent of her hair, the powder silk of her skin, the words she'd whispered against the distant roar of waves as he'd brought her closer to each climax.

He wished he could promise Nina more—particularly after April's wedding yesterday. The day had stirred feelings inside him he hadn't known existed... and wasn't entirely sure he wanted to acknowledge. The truest part of him didn't want a heavy relationship—moving in, plans for the future, worrying about whether that future would pan out. If putting so much into hauling this island out of the red was a risk, to his mind getting serious with a woman was like putting a blowtorch to a gas leak. "Serious" led to "marriage," which led to children—and kids deserved the best from both parents. He wasn't ready to think about that yet—wasn't ready to take that risk even with someone as special as Nina.

He walked into the café's alfresco area and indicated to the *maître-d'* that he'd seat himself. Halfway to a vacant table near the railing, he recognised a woman in a floral shift.

Mrs Emily Flounders, from Sydney's North Shore, beckoned him over. "Why, Mr Steele, is that you? We met at the children's charity dinner last month."

Gabe smiled, nodded. "Mrs Flounders." Mr Flounders lowered his paper and Gabe leaned across to shake his hand. "Sir."

Mrs Flounders laced glittering fingers under her double chin. "Things going well, I hope?"

"Very. Thank you."

"We brought Linley along. You remember Linley?" She tipped forward. "Our daughter? You spoke with her at the dinner."

He didn't remember—which said a lot. "Of course. Please give Linley my regards."

A moment later he drew in his chair and spotted Nina, breezing out from the café's interior. He hadn't noticed so much on the other staff, but that uniform *could* do with a brush-up in design—not shorter, nor sexier, nor even more stylish. Just…more colour, more shape, more *oomph*.

Nina screeched to a stop when she spotted him. After sending him a curious *what are you up to?* look, she crossed to the Flounders' table.

Gabriel absently perused the menu, glancing across every few seconds, strangely nervous for her, but proud of her too. She could have taken the easy way out, accepted his help in finding her a suitable job back in Sydney that she'd enjoy. Instead she was here, travelling that road of hers to its natural conclusion— wherever that might be.

Nina was taking the Flounders' order, but it didn't seem to be going well. Mrs Flounders' cheeks were ruddy, and Nina kept crossing out what she'd written. Concerned, Gabriel set his menu aside at the same time as Nina hurried off to the kitchen to place the order. Mrs Flounders waved over the *maître-d'*.

Gabriel couldn't hear the exchange, but it was clear the older woman was complaining about Nina. Mrs Flounders was a pretentious show pony who loved attention. Maybe Nina had had trouble deciphering the doyenne's demands, but that hardly deserved a complaint.

When the *maître-d'* strode away, Gabriel scraped back his chair and followed. Through the round window in the swinging door that led to the kitchen he saw him ripping verbal shreds off Nina. His arms were waving. Gabriel made out a few words...stupid... incompetent...but more obvious was the man's scathing tone.

Nina, however, didn't flinch. She merely looked her boss in the eye and shrugged her shoulders back. Gabriel imagined her topaz eyes glistening, her thumping heart jammed in her throat.

Not on his shift.

Gabriel crashed through the door. He was ready to tell the *maître-d'* to take a hike, but pulled back when he heard Nina's level voice.

"I will not apologise," she was saying. "I did nothing wrong. If anyone should say I'm sorry, that woman should say it to me. And she could throw in a dozen more apologies to the other staff she's put through her wringer since she sat down an hour ago."

The *maître-d'* was clearly shocked. "You are not here to argue—"

"I'm not arguing. I'm simply stating that there's a big difference between making sure the guests are happy and insisting that your staff smile while they lick their boots three times a day."

A general positive murmur went up around the interested kitchen staff. The head chef nodded to his assistant. A waitress had stopped in her tracks, her eyes wide with disbelief and admiration.

The *maître-d'* glowered in their general direction, then redirected his spite towards Nina. "You will go back out there and apologise to the Flounders, then you will attempt to take their order and do it *correctly* this time!"

"I took it correctly the first time, the second time *and* the third," Nina insisted. "That woman is nothing but a contrary snob who thinks it's her God-given right to demean people she considers beneath her."

With a condescending air, the *maître-d'* crossed his arms. "You foolish girl. You know *nothing* of how the other half live."

Her chin kicked higher. "I know more than you'd ever believe."

Gabriel remembered how a younger Nina had once treated him—as if he should lick *her* boots. She'd come a long way. All these years and finally he really thought she got it.

But it was time to bring this show to an end. The other staff were beyond agitated. He didn't want a rebellion on his hands, but he couldn't dismiss Nina—although he would have to talk soundly with her later. While the man she slept with applauded her guts, the businessman standing here needed to repair any damage.

He moved forward. Nina's jaw dropped when she saw him.

"You're having the rest of the day off," he told the *maître-d',* who reddened more.

"B-but the guests?" he jabbered.

Gabriel relieved him of the menus he held. "I'll look after the guests."

Indignant, the *maître-d'* stood on his toes. "Forgive me, sir, but you have no experience in this field."

"Guess I'd better learn."

As the kitchen staff raised their brows and murmured

more, Gabriel nodded towards the door. The *maître-d'* huffed and strode out.

Nina was tugging at his sleeve. "Gabriel, I need to talk to you."

"We'll talk after this shift," he said, dying to snatch a kiss. He loved her when she was determined. Loved it when she spoke her mind.

And rather than comply she headed for a door—a backroom where a store of food was kept. She hooked a finger for him to follow, and Gabriel's pulse-rate ramped up.

Okay. If she was that insistent they be alone, he guessed he could spare a moment…or two.

He put the menus aside and followed her. The murmurs outside increased before he shut the door. Not needing an invitation now they were alone, he brought her snug against him, felt a surge of desire flare and build. Now he had her pressed close it was going to prove beyond difficult to let her go.

He brushed his lips over hers and, closing his eyes, groaned with unbridled pleasure. "You were sensational out there."

"Gabriel—"

He pulled marginally back. "But I can't have you dressing down superiors in front of the staff. It doesn't look right."

"*Gabe,* listen to me. I've found another job."

His thoughts screeched to a stop. Dumbfounded, he examined her open gaze. "You *what?*"

"A lady I worked with at *Shimmer* told me about a new magazine starting up. I e-mailed my résumé a couple of days ago and this morning the editor e-mailed back. We talked on the phone and…" Her shoulders came down. "She wants me to start next week. I'll be features editor and second in charge."

He butted his shoulder against the wall as his mind clicked over.

Right. Okay. He should be happy for her. Should be smiling.

"That's…great. Wonderful." He exhaled, struck a hand through his hair. "Next week, huh?"

"I'm leaving tomorrow."

His mind and body gridlocked. "As soon as that?" He'd decided he was going to stay on for a while. He hadn't decided how long exactly. He'd planned on telling Nina after her shift. He'd imagined she'd be happy.

"When she told me I had the job," Nina went on, "can you believe I was actually torn? I had something to finish here—I wasn't entirely sure what—so I said I'd call back if my answer was yes." She shook her head as she sighed. "Now, after that scene—when I know I'd only done my job well… That's it for me. I'm done. I don't want to be subjected to this kind of pompous elitism ever again."

Gabriel's mind caught up with his emotions and delayed relief trickled through him. She might be leaving the island, but… "We can hook up again in Sydney."

"That sounds wonderful, except…"

He frowned. "Except what?"

Searching his eyes, she eased out a long breath. "I was feeling so lost and alone…it was what I'd been dreaming of before you came along—lapping up luxury for just a day or two. This time with you has brought back so many memories. Safe memories from when I was young and my family were all together." She rested her palm against his chest. "But that time's over. That's not me any more. I've changed. I don't want to try and fit back into that world. The world of pretentious Mrs Flounders. I'd feel more of a fake than I did being a waitress." Her eyes pleaded with him to understand. "You've made so much of yourself. You deserve all this. But that's *you*, not me. Not any more."

He held her hand against his chest and scoffed. She was making this bigger than it needed to be.

"Nina, we're not doing anything drastic." Like making things permanent. "We're just seeing each other." Sleeping together. "You can still have your life and carry on doing that."

Her throat bobbed on a big swallow and her eyes began to fill. "No matter what life throws my way, I know now I'll adapt. I'll survive. I'll *grow*. But that doesn't mean I want to intentionally put myself in harm's way. I care about you, Gabriel. I care so much it frightens me." Her face softened. "I've never been in love before."

His heart stopped beating. He swallowed involuntarily, then, totally taken aback, coughed out a laugh. "We've known each other a *week*."

"*This* time." Her eyes glistened. "If I agree to see you when we get back you'll end up hurting me, and it'll be my fault for not pulling back now while I still can."

Suddenly the room felt smaller. Where it had been cosy when they'd first entered, now the space felt squashed. The scent of spices and sauces made him want to wheeze. Made him want to clear his throat.

He blindly found the doorknob at his back. "We'll discuss this later."

"Will that change anything?"

He'd be frank.

"If you're talking about long-term, about marriage… no, it won't. And you know enough about me not to ask why." With marriage came expectations, came children. He'd rather not be a father at all than risk being a bad or an absent one. Boys needed their father—one hundred percent and every day.

She cupped his cheek with a caring hand. "You're so committed to this project. You have so much riding on its success. You don't need me getting in the way. You don't need nagging when you're too busy for personal."

His hand tightened on her shoulder before it slid down her arm. He leant back against the door. He felt as if he'd been knocked out in the final round. He hated to admit it, but everything she said made sense. The scenario she'd just given had pretty much been the way most of his so-called relationships had turned out in the past. He'd thought Nina was different, but maybe her added allure was because she'd been so proud and so darn hard to keep.

He might not love her, but he did respect her, and he certainly didn't want to hurt her.

He closed his eyes, saw the only logical answer and forced himself to accept it.

Exhaling, he opened his eyes and nodded. "You're right. If you were my sister, I'd be telling you to run."

She frowned. "This isn't about Anthony."

"No, this is about you being you and me being me."

She was moving on and he wasn't ready to make that move with her. He didn't know that he ever would be.

CHAPTER FOURTEEN

LATER that day, after Gabriel had walked a few miles down the beach, he strode back to the bungalow and immersed himself in figures. Piles of columns and statistics and any other numbers that might help to obliterate that God-awful scene in the café with Nina Petrelle.

There'd been a note on the counter. Nina was staying with her mate back at the staff quarters tonight.

He scrunched up the paper, flicked it into the trash. When night fell, he cracked open a beer and reclined in a deckchair out on the balcony. With the Mikano restaurant's piano tinkling in over the warm air, he watched the waves roll endlessly in, then roll just as endlessly out. He slept not a wink. When a peaceful dawn broke, sienna-gold on the quiet horizon, his eyes were gritty and his throat ached.

He believed he could change Nina's mind. He knew what to say, how to touch, where to kiss, so she couldn't say no. But, as much as the beast inside urged him to persuade her to continue their affair after she returned to Sydney, he simply couldn't be that selfish and hurt her that way.

As he'd said—she was right. His past with women was proof. Nina would only end up hurt.

She wanted his respect and he *did* respect her—her courage, her humour and integrity. But respect and love were two different things. If she was frightened about how much she cared for him, he wasn't too comfortable with his emotions either.

He'd told her his life was too busy to accommodate the kind of commitment she was wanted. But through these long, lonely hours he'd admitted that was a lie. The simple truth was he didn't *want* to be tied down. But it went deeper than that. He didn't want to commit because he didn't need to worry about whether he was good enough. Whether he could provide enough—emotionally, financially, physically.

His mother hadn't given his father a chance and young Gabe had been the one to lose out. He'd come to terms with his mother's choices. He'd forgiven her long ago. But he had Faith and her gentle wise ways to thank for that.

Faith had said, no matter what, he could be anything he wanted to be. But in a dark hidden place, he knew why he'd never let himself get close to any woman.

He didn't believe in that kind of love. And until recently he hadn't found that conviction to be a problem.

At 7 a.m. he showered, dressed, and made his way to the jetty. An hour later he stood when Nina approached, wheeling one suitcase behind her. The ferry-cat to the mainland left in twenty minutes. Twenty minutes and then…

Would he ever see her again?

She didn't seem surprised to see him. Her eyes looked as red as his felt, and it was all he could do not to tell her this was crazy. This didn't have to end.

Instead he remembered her pleas, his long, insightful night, and handed over a tiger shell.

"This is for your nephew." He placed the shiny tawny- and brown-dotted shell in her hand. "Put your ear to the opening and you hear the ocean."

She listened, smiled, and then lowered the shell. "Thank you," she said. "Thanks for everything you've done."

He dropped his gaze and then found her eyes again. "Nina, I did some soul-searching last night."

Her gaze sharpened. "And?"

"I want you to be everything you can be."

In a heartbeat her eyes edged with tears and, although she set her mouth, her bottom lip still trembled. It was the hardest thing he'd ever done, holding back from gathering her close, kissing her brow and telling her… what?

He'd already said he cared. He cared more for her than anyone he'd known. More than Faith, more than his father or Anthony. It was a different kind of emotion. A consuming sensation that affected every inch of him…head, but more so heart. And yet he couldn't tell her what she needed to hear.

So what was the use of tormenting himself? Or her? Why had he come?

"Good luck with your work here," she said.

He blinked against the emotion stinging behind his nose. "Good luck with the new job."

A tear fell from the corner of her eye before she bounced onto tiptoe and stole a kiss from his cheek. Then she was gone, striding off down the jetty, boarding the cat and not looking back.

Soon it began to shower. The shower turned into sheets of rain. After an hour, Gabriel walked home.

He knew he could get Diamond Shores back on its feet. He was well on track now, thanks to Nina and the other staff's suggestions. She was right. No one needed to lick anyone's boots—not in his childhood and not now. He'd make the changes that needed to be made. He'd make the fortune he'd always wanted. He'd prove himself. Reach the top.

Yet all he could think about was how lucky some guy in Nina's future would be and how, without her in his life, he might as well be broke.

CHAPTER FIFTEEN

NINA had been back in Sydney two weeks, and had started her new job at *Real Woman's Life* magazine a few days ago.

She'd fallen straight into the work and had hit it off instantly with her fellow staff. Best was the feeling that she finally fitted somewhere again. Her life was definitely on the upswing. Yet there was a hidden part of her that felt more lost than ever.

Sitting alone on a quiet stretch of Manly Beach, with a chorus of kookaburras heralding in a clear new day, Nina pushed to her feet, dusted off her shorts and headed for the water.

Once she'd loved coming here…laughable attempts at beach volleyball with her friends, devouring great summer reads while the sun warmed her skin. Now blue skies, white sand and the mighty tumble of surf only reminded her of Gabriel.

Almost to the water, she stopped as her insides clenched and tears brimmed in her eyes.

She'd tried to shake off the malady…late-night movies, visits with Jill and Codie, reconnecting with mates and former colleagues. Yet every waking moment his smile seemed to live in her mind. Dazzling. Seductive.

Her dreams were even more disturbing. Sometimes she woke up believing his bone-melting embrace was real. The memory of his night kisses teased her until she thought she might go mad.

She had to talk with him, tell him she'd been wrong, that she was willing to take whatever he could give. Last night the ache in her stomach had been so bad she'd picked up the phone, ready to beg him to take her back.

What did she have to lose? The tragedy she'd hoped to avoid had come. Her heart was broken. Cracked in two. Her professional life was soaring, but on a personal, lovesick note, she doubted she could sink any lower.

And it was that sorry realisation that kept her from crumbling completely. From making another gigantic mistake.

If she called Gabriel and pitched herself back into their affair she would only fall *more* in love. She would be even more heartbroken when they said goodbye again. In not so many words, on that last day, Gabriel had told her to run.

He knew who he was…a playboy millionaire who had success and little else on his mind. But he cared for her. When she lay awake in the midnight hours, staring at the ceiling, she told herself he cared for her more than any woman he'd been with.

Still, he'd let her go.

She *couldn't* take back all she'd said to him. Couldn't let him know she was willing to have her heart decimated again. She might not have Gabriel Steele's love, but she could at least keep his respect.

And so, once she'd gone around that circle of logic a thousand times, she stayed her course. She longed for Gabriel's smile, his touch. But she kept her pain to herself.

But then came the next dilemma.

Would she ever feel whole again…the wonderful, glowing, cherished way she'd felt when she'd been with him? When she looked in the mirror each morning and saw the opacity in her eyes she couldn't imagine feeling that vibrant again.

As cool laces of water washed around her bare feet, Nina wondered where and what her life would be ten years from now. She'd always thought she would find Mr Wonderful, her true soul mate, and she *had*. Love had come at the most unlikely time, when every other aspect of her life had been turned upside down and pulled inside out. But finding love wasn't keeping love. One week after meeting Mr Wonderful she'd lost her love for good.

She gazed out at the Pacific Ocean, glittering with dawn's gentle jewels, and hugged herself as a cool sea breeze combed her hair.

The question she'd asked herself lately hadn't been, *Who am I?* It was *Why am I? Why am I here?*

Why do I matter?

She came up with reasons. Good ones. Reasons that counted. And yet without Gabriel to talk with…to laugh with…to love…those reasons never seemed anywhere near important enough.

Ahead, a bottle lay half buried in the sand. An unusual bottle—bright pink, with a spray of flowers painted on one side. Curious, she collected it and rubbed the wet sand from the glass.

She stopped. Looked harder.

Paper was scrolled up inside.

A message in a bottle.

A wistful smile lifted the corners of her mouth.

On the night of April's wedding Gabriel had asked her what she might write on such a note.

Nina closed her eyes, lifted her face to the northern sky and whispered… *'Wish you were here.'*

Remembering her first vision of him on that cliff, she swallowed the tears backed up in her throat, screwed off the cork and shook the paper out. Unravelling the note, she saw the words were handwritten and slightly smudged. Only two words, and they read:

Turn around.

She blinked several times before tendrils of understanding gripped high around her throat and a flash of heat rushed over her skin. Her head was light and every hair on her scalp was standing on end by the time she did what the note asked. Slowly she edged around, and…

Gabriel! He was standing right there before her, as if he'd materialised out of thin air.

Her shaky grasp on the bottle slipped, but he caught it, as well as her hands, before it hit the ground.

He looked ten times more masculine and handsome than she'd remembered. Those ice-blue eyes burned into hers, warming her all the way through. A raspy shadow darkened his prominent jaw. She loved grazing her palm up the rough of his mid-morning beard.

Or rather she *had* loved doing that.

Nina wondered if her face showed even a tenth of her emotions. She wanted to run away, to beg him to stay. Tell him how desperately she wanted him to hold her.

But she didn't need to ask. Gabriel's strong arms wrapped around her and, still in shock, she didn't resist when he drew her near.

"I remember it all," he said against her ear as she

trembled and he stroked her back. "As if every moment were logged in my brain beneath a magnifying glass. How you chew the end of your pencil when you pore over a crossword. How your foot taps when you listen to your favourite song. How you feel beneath me. Feel around me."

Her voice pushed past the nerves knotted in her throat. "Gabriel…what are you doing here?"

He stepped back and found her gaze.

"Since you left I haven't stopped asking myself whether I could truly keep you satisfied. Day and night, it pounded at my brain. I wanted to come to you, wanted you back, but I couldn't stomach the idea of not measuring up."

He inhaled and his gaze focused more. "Years ago, I vowed I would never be responsible for helping to create another broken home. Then, out of the blue, the answer came to me."

Unable to help herself, she filed her fingers through the sides of his clean dark hair, wondering how she'd lived so long without his touch. Raw hope pushed like a fist against her chest, but she didn't want to jump ahead. Didn't want to hope too much.

"You wanted to discover who you were," he went on, his voice intense and deep. "Let me tell you who you are to me. You're the person I can face any battle with. You're headstrong and beyond beautiful. You're like no one I've ever known. Nina, you're the woman I love and will love for ever. And I'm the man who prays you can forgive me for not realising that sooner and love me back." He found her hands and clasped them to his chest, and that beautiful light she adored shone up in his eyes. "I want to help create a *happy* family. *Our* family. Nina, say you'll marry me."

She felt locked to the spot. The ocean and the sky and the kookaburra calls receded, until she was only aware of her throbbing heartbeat and the deep sincerity in his eyes. Over her clogged throat, she choked out what had played over in her mind these past weeks. He wasn't the only one who'd been asking questions.

"Gabe, you said you didn't want to get married."

She didn't want to believe it—didn't want to think he'd be that cruel—but she had to know if this was another seduction game meant to get her back in his bed.

He tipped her chin up and gazed into her soul. "I was waiting for the right woman, and I can't believe I almost let her go." His arms went around her again. "I want to live the rest of my life with you. Have children together and be there for them every day. I want to sit and watch the sunrise with you fifty years from now. Tell me you want that too." His brow lowered to rest upon hers. "Tell me you still feel the same way."

Her chest squeezed until she could barely breathe. Of course she still loved him. Now that she'd fallen, she couldn't imagine *not* loving him. He sounded so passionate, so focused, but there was something else she needed to say. The part of her that was weeping with happiness was telling her to keep quiet. She wanted to accept his proposal—she'd *dreamed* about it since the day they'd said goodbye—but she couldn't simply push aside what she knew to be true.

"What about your life? Gabriel, I don't want to live in a world of black-tie dinners every other night. I can't be a *real housewife*." She couldn't be a rich kept woman, with too much time and money on her hands. After all she'd been through, that skin simply wouldn't fit.

"Our life doesn't have to be like that. We don't have to have anyone or anything in our life we don't want to have there. That obstacle's not enough to keep us apart. Nothing is." His determined eyes searched hers. "This connection is real. For ever. We'll *make* it work. Believe it, Nina. Believe it the way I do and nothing else will matter."

A flood of emotion bubbled up. She wanted to laugh. To *cry*. She choked out the words. "You really think so?"

"I love you…and I won't let anything stand in our way."

His head slanted over hers, and when their lips met and his masterful heat and confidence infused her she went to jelly and gave up her arguments. With all her heart, with everything she'd ever been and ever would be, she wanted this. Wanted him.

With tears spilling down her cheeks, she twined her arms around his neck and hitched back a happy sob as his lips reluctantly left hers.

There was supposed to be one special person in this world for everyone.

That's why I'm here, she told herself, feeling the full depth of that truth. *I'm here to love you.* Not above and beyond everything else, but to strengthen and enrich everything else she was now and was destined to be.

"We'll go straight to a store and pick out a ring," he murmured, his voice thick with love and pride.

But as his eyes glistened into hers—so full of conviction and faith—she flexed her fingers into his shirt. "I'd rather go straight home and get reacquainted."

"Why wait to get home?"

Without warning, he hoisted her up, a hand either side of her waist, and swung her around in a giddy, exhilarating circle. Alive with hope. Bursting with passion. Nina's heart was so full she wanted all the world to know this kind of happiness.

They were laughing and out of breath by the time he folded down with her onto the wet sand. As a shallow wave washed in and scalloped around them, she lay over his chest and whispered, "I love you so much. I wanted to call you so much."

His gaze roamed her face and he smiled. "I'm here now."

"Do you think we were in love all those years ago?"

A playful frown pinched his brow. "You were only fourteen."

"Juliet was fourteen."

"I'm more interested in writing our own love story."

He cradled her head, and Nina melted when his mouth claimed hers again.

As a rising swell of trust and passion consumed and lifted her up, in her heart Nina knew just three things:

The very best of her life had just begun…

She wished this kiss could last for ever…

And, as much as she loved this man—and she loved him to the infinite depths of her soul—Gabriel Turner Steele loved her more.

MILLS & BOON

MODERN
Heat™

On sale 19th March 2010

UNTAMEABLE ROGUE
by Kelly Hunter

Businesswoman Madeline Delacourte has no time and no need for a man in her life…until she meets Luke Bennett. Madeline knows she's playing with fire. He is as roguish as he is seductive, and if she unleashes this bad boy's passion she'd better learn how to tame it – otherwise it's her who'll end up getting burnt!

On sale 2nd April 2010

WEDDING NIGHT WITH A STRANGER
by Anna Cleary

Sebastian Nikosto hadn't known what to expect from his contract wife-to-be, but certainly not the beautiful Ariadne, or the instant heat between them! Perhaps there might be an upside to this ridiculous arrangement? But once the bartered bride's been bedded, it seems neither party is in such a hurry to annul the marriage as planned…

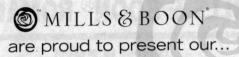

MILLS & BOON® ROMANCE

is proud to present

Jewels of the Desert

Deserts, diamonds and destiny!

The Kingdom of Quishari: two rulers, with hearts as hard as the rugged landscape they reign over, are in need of Desert Queens…

When they offer convenient proposals, will they discover doing your duty doesn't have to mean ignoring your heart?

Sheikh Rashid and his twin brother Sheikh Khalid are looking for brides in…

ACCIDENTALLY THE SHEIKH'S WIFE
And
MARRYING THE SCARRED SHEIKH
by Barbara McMahon
in April 2010

millsandboon.co.uk Community

Join Us!

The Community is the perfect place to meet and chat to kindred spirits who love books and reading as much as you do, but it's also the place to:

- **Get the inside scoop from authors about their latest books**
- **Learn how to write a romance book with advice from our editors**
- **Help us to continue publishing the best in women's fiction**
- **Share your thoughts on the books we publish**
- **Befriend other users**

Forums: Interact with each other as well as authors, editors and a whole host of other users worldwide.

Blogs: Every registered community member has their own blog to tell the world what they're up to and what's on their mind.

Book Challenge: We're aiming to read 5,000 books and have joined forces with The Reading Agency in our inaugural Book Challenge.

Profile Page: Showcase yourself and keep a record of your recent community activity.

Social Networking: We've added buttons at the end of every post to share via digg, Facebook, Google, Yahoo, technorati and de.licio.us.

www.millsandboon.co.uk